THE MISSING SCHOOLGIRLS

A 1930s Detective Mystery

Peter Zander-Howell

Copyright © 2025 Peter Zander-Howell

All rights reserved.

Certain well-known historical persons are mentioned in this work. All other characters and events portrayed in this book are fictitious, and any similarity to real persons, alive or dead, is coincidental and not intended by the author. Real-world locations in this book may have been slightly altered.

No part of this book may be reproduced, or stored in a retrieval system, or transmitted in any form or by any means, electronic, mechanical, photocopying, recording, or otherwise, without the express permission of the publisher.

ISBN - 9798306980614

CONTENTS

Title Page
Copyright
THE PRINCIPAL CHARACTERS

CHAPTER 1	1
CHAPTER 2	12
CHAPTER 3	19
CHAPTER 4	39
CHAPTER 5	55
CHAPTER 6	74
CHAPTER 7	91
CHAPTER 8	105
CHAPTER 9	120
CHAPTER 10	137
CHAPTER 11	151
CHAPTER 12	170
CHAPTER 13	192
CHAPTER 14	208
Books By This Author	225

THE PRINCIPAL CHARACTERS

WILLOWBANK SCHOOL - NOVEMBER 1938
(Note - to avoid confusion only names mentioned in the story are shown)

Headmistress - Miss Lucy Armstrong

Lovelace House
Housemistress - Miss Fleming
House Tutor - Miss Jacqueline Bennett

Wollstonecraft House
Housemistress - A N Other
House Tutor - Miss Laura Filby

Burdett-Coutts House
Housemistress - Mrs Cerys Redpath
             + Mr Brian Redpath
House Tutor - Miss Ciara McCullough

Pankhurst House
Housemistress - Mrs April Harvey
             + Mr Jonathan Harvey
House Tutor - A N Other

Nightingale House
Housemistress - Miss Patricia Trelawney
House Tutor- A N Other

Fry House
Housemistress - Miss Laura Jekyll
House Tutor - Miss Patricia Finlay

Austen House

Housemistress - Miss Danielle Ovenden
House Tutor - A N Other

Somerville House
Housemistress - Mrs Eleanor Livermore
    + Dr Keith Livermore
House Tutor - A N Other

12 other teachers including Miss Felicity Townsend, living outside the school.

School Secretary - Miss Angela Spencer
Bursar - Mr William Dodds
Groundsmen - Painter
    - Green
Odd-job men - Dalby
    - Bailey

The Missing Children:
Miss Aaliyah Hammadani (father - Mr Yussef Hammadani)
Lady Megan Innes-Fielding (father - The Earl of Trimley)

Other key children:
Leila Iqbal
Nadiyya Qadir

Sundry cooks, maids, etc.

The key Police officers:

From New Scotland Yard:

Detective Chief Inspector David Adair
Detective Inspector Barry Davison
Detective Sergeant James Borthwick
Detective Sergeant Patrick Gemmill

From the Kent Constabulary:

The Chief Constable - Colonel Rupert Hardy
Superintendent Paul Waller
Inspector Jeremy Hatrick
Sergeant Ellis

From the Essex Constabulary:

Inspector Goddard

CHAPTER 1

Monday 14th November, 1938

"Enter," bawled Inspector Jeremy Hatrick. He eyed without enthusiasm the young uniformed constable who came into the room.

"Well?" he growled. "I should have gone home nearly two hours ago, and you've come to keep me here even longer."

"Sorry to disturb you sir, but that Miss Spencer from Willowbank has just been on the telephone again. She says a second girl seems to be missing."

"To paraphrase Lady Bracknell, Carter. To lose one child may be regarded as a misfortune; to lose two looks like carelessness. Have we sent anyone to the school yet?"

"Not yet, sir. Sergeant Ellis has only just come on duty, and he is going when he's had a cup of tea."

Hatrick grunted. "Tea before he's even started his shift? All right. Give him this latest information. Pound to a penny these kids have just gone off somewhere and lost track of time. Did this woman – I assume she's the Headmistress – say they were together when they were last seen?"

"I don't think she knew, sir. Apparently she is the School Secretary, calling on behalf of her boss."

"I see. The matter not important enough for the Head to report this herself. All right, Carter, clear off and leave me in peace."

With some justification it was widely believed in the police station that the Inspector deliberately cultivated a grumpy persona, while in reality being a softie, and Carter left the room smiling to himself. He made his way up to the canteen, where he found Sergeant Ellis draining the last few drops from his teacup. In a few words the Constable passed on the latest news. Predictably, his superior snorted derisively. Not being quite so erudite as the Inspector, he didn't quote Oscar Wilde, but what he did mutter showed that he shared Hatrick's view that sending police to the school was a complete waste of time.

"These kids will have been found before I arrive, Carter, I'd put money on that," was his parting remark as he trotted off down the stairs.

Ellis said much the same thing to his fellow-Sergeant on the front desk as he passed by on his way out to his car.

Fifteen minutes later, he turned into the drive of one of the most exclusive girls' schools in the country. Willowbank had been founded in the 1880s, actually a couple of years before the better-known Roedean in the next county. It occupied what had been built as a grand mansion in the early eighteenth century. The last surviving member of the original family – a female – with nobody to pass the great house on to, decided to create a trust with the purpose of founding and running a school for girls. Plans were put in place and polished, helped by a very considerable injection of capital from the benefactress. Eventually, only a matter of months before the good lady died, the school opened.

Credit for the inspired selection of a young and energetic Headmistress, and for all the earlier planning, was owed to the Trust's Committee. The members had been appointed by the benefactress herself, who had persuaded a number of her influential friends and acquaintances to participate. The original chairman was the Lord Lieutenant of the county, and the six other members were perhaps even more celebrated – a senior cabinet minister, two members of the House of Lords and the wife of a third, a High Court judge, and the wife of a prominent newspaper editor.

The school had quickly become known, and within five years of its foundation was already ranked among the top in the country.

Sergeant Ellis knew nothing of this history, and had never had occasion to pass through the great entrance gates and the twin lodges before, but as he drew nearer to the school he realised that the original stately home had been extended several times over the years. In fact each of the various extensions and modifications – particularly the huge matching wings erected to either side of the original façade – had been executed quite tastefully, but Ellis, not being interested in architecture, didn't even consider the point.

He parked not far from the front door of the original house, which still seemed to be the entrance to the school. There was an old-fashioned iron bell-pull beside the door, and he gave this a good tug. A muffled jangle from inside confirmed that the mechanism was still in working order. Within seconds the great oak door was opened by a diminutive woman who had apparently anticipated his arrival.

"Thank you for coming, Sergeant; I'm Angela Spencer, the School Secretary. May I have your name so I can introduce you to Miss Armstrong?

Ellis told her who he was, and then followed the woman for some distance along corridors. Eventually they stopped, and Miss Spencer tapped on a door marked 'Headmistress'. Opening it without waiting for a response, she led Ellis into what had obviously been some sort of grand living room in the original house.

"This is Sergeant Ellis, Lucy," announced the Secretary; "Sergeant, this is our Head, Miss Armstrong."

"Welcome to Willowbank, Sergeant," said the Head, a tall woman of about fifty who was wearing a grey two-piece suit. She removed her gold-rimmed spectacles as she stood to greet him. "Do take a seat. We don't have any time to waste, but can we get you some tea while we talk?"

"No, thank you ma'am," replied Ellis, "I had a cup not twenty minutes ago."

"All right, Angela, you go and see if there is anything happening – keep me informed, of course.

"I've only been here a few months, Sergeant, but I'm told that we have never had a visit from the police," said the Head after the Secretary had gone. "No burglary, or anything that would need your help. Today is a very unfortunate precedent. You received the message about a second missing girl, I presume?"

"Yes, ma'am. The second report came in minutes before I left the station."

"Well, this situation has never occurred before. I'm not given to panicking, but I am certainly becoming very concerned. Let me tell you what we have been doing.

"As soon as we found the second child was missing, I gathered ten members of staff and ten prefects, and put them into pairs. Each pair was allocated a search area, with overlaps. The main part of the school has been thoroughly searched, as have all eight boarding houses. A few minutes before you arrived, the teams searching the outlying buildings – the swimming pool block, potting sheds, and so on – reported back. There is no sign of the missing girls. The pair looking in and around the sports pavilion haven't returned yet. The fact that it is dark is a serious handicap, of course.

"What can the police do to help us?"

Ellis hesitated. He was still sure that there would be some rational explanation, and that the children would soon turn up, no doubt embarrassed at the fuss they had caused. He temporised.

"Can you tell me what they would or should have been doing in the time between when they were last seen and now?"

"Yes, of course. Classes finished today at four o'clock, give or take a few minutes. Crucially, each girl was present for her last lesson.

"After school, the girls are then free until the evening meal, taken in their houses at half past six. Some will just return to their house straight away; others might go to the school library, or to the swimming pool – but that isn't open in the dark. In the summer some would go for a walk around the grounds – and there are various games options in the summer too, such as tennis. They can do what they like as long as they remain within the grounds.

"In each of the boarding houses, the girls can socialise in the common room, but each of those missing is old enough to have her own single study to which she can retreat if she so wishes – although the studies are large enough to invite in two or even three friends.

"Anyway, the girls were missing for the evening meal. The two relevant Housemistresses noticed someone was absent, but initially didn't take much notice.

"Now what may be the crucial point is this. Obviously, the parents of children here are not poor. Some are very rich indeed. It may or may not be significant – I hope it isn't – but the two missing girls come from very, very affluent homes."

Miss Armstrong paused, and looked hard at Ellis.

"They also come from very influential families."

"Can you give me their names, ma'am?" Ellis took out his pocket book and a pencil.

"Yes. Lady Megan Innes-Fielding, daughter of the Earl of Trimley – he owns a sizeable chunk of Suffolk, and is also Chairman of Taylor's bank. She is fourteen.

"The second is Aaliyah Hammadani, also fourteen. Closely related to Middle Eastern royalty. Oil, you know. Her father is currently in this country negotiating something or other – he came to visit his daughter last Sunday. I should tell you that he is on close terms with both the Prime Minister and His Majesty the King.

"Now, you haven't asked, but I can say that there is no apparent friendship between Megan and Aaliyah. In other words, it's unlikely that they went off together. They are not in the same house, and although they are the same age they are not in the same class, and enquiries I've made suggest they are no more than acquaintances.

"I'll repeat my question. What can the police do?"

Ellis felt inadequate. He thought rapidly about what could be done, and apart from broadcasting an appeal, nothing came to mind. Yet there was now a possibility that this was a case – or rather two cases – of kidnapping. Or worse. His confusion was apparent from his face.

"I think you still need to be persuaded that the police must act. Let me explain further." Miss Armstrong now delivered two telling blows.

"First, in the next few minutes I shall have to contact the parents concerned. Needless to say I am not looking forward to that. But I shall also have to contact every other parent somehow, by telegram, I suppose, to inform them of what has happened before they read about it in the newspapers. After I start doing that, all hell will break out. We have two parents who are government ministers, and a score or so other MPs. There are also KCs, judges, millionaire industrialists, newspaper editors, and many other parents in equally influential positions. Be in no doubt that the pressure on your constabulary – and indeed on me – will be immense.

"Earlier, I said we have had no visits from

the police. As far as business visits are concerned, that was true. However, one particular officer comes here regularly. He takes his granddaughter out to tea on every third Sunday. That man is Colonel Hardy – your Chief Constable."

Sergeant Ellis was squirming after the Head's first point, and as she finished speaking he stood up.

"I need to contact my Inspector at once, ma'am. Perhaps I could use a telephone in your Secretary's office?"

"Yes. But her extension and mine are on the same line, and I shall need that more or less constantly for the rest of today, so be very quick. She is in the next room – go through that connecting door.

"If I'm on the telephone when you or your superiors need more information, or you have anything to report, find my Deputy, Mrs Livermore – she is the Housemistress in Somerville House – or the Bursar, Mr Dodds, whose office is the other side of Angela's."

Ellis quickly passed into the next office. Miss Spencer was talking to two females – one evidently a teacher and the other a senior pupil. He was in time to hear the teacher report that they had found no sign of any of the missing girls.

"You're the last, then," said the Secretary. "I'll pass this on to Miss Armstrong. Oh dear, oh dear."

The two others looked at the Sergeant

curiously as they left the room, but neither spoke.

"Miss Armstrong says I may use your telephone," said Ellis. She doesn't want me to take very long as she has urgent calls to make herself."

"Sit at my desk, Sergeant. I'll just pass on this latest information."

Picking up the telephone, Ellis asked to be connected to the police station. Within a minute he was speaking to his Inspector, and two minutes after that he had conveyed the salient points to his superior.

Hatrick was silent for a moment, and then released a few unprintable words.

"All right, Ellis. I'll find the Super, but obviously he'll get on to the Chief immediately. Stay where you are."

The Sergeant explained that the school telephone line was soon likely to be permanently engaged.

"Not to worry. We can always tell the operator to cut in. But chances are we'll be sending reinforcements, although God knows what they'll be able to do."

Hatrick hung up his handset, picked up his hat, and went to find the Superintendent.

Ellis was replacing his own receiver just as Miss Spencer returned. She saw his action, and turned back to speak through the still-open door.

"The Sergeant is off the line now, Lucy."

She came back into the room, closing the interconnecting door behind her. Ellis relinquished his chair, and stood looking unhappy.

"What is going to happen?" asked the Secretary.

Ellis shrugged his shoulders. "The matter is being passed up the chain very rapidly. I gather our Chief Constable has a connection with the school, so no doubt he'll be briefed within minutes. We'll have to see what he decides to do."

Miss Spencer left the room to do something else, leaving Ellis alone. He wondered whether he should start questioning anyone – other girls in the various classes or in the relevant houses, but the scale of the exercise deterred him. Also, he didn't really have any idea as to what questions to ask. He sat down in a chair beside the desk, and tried to imagine what Miss Armstrong would be saying to the parents – and what the parents of the missing girls would be saying to her.

CHAPTER 2

Hatrick found that, as he had anticipated, the Superintendent had gone home, and so returned to his office where he picked up the telephone. He was able to contact his superior within a very few minutes. The Super mouthed a number of the same words that the Inspector had used, but after a few seconds the tirade stopped.

All right, Hatrick, I'll try to contact the Chief. Stay by your desk."

It was now the Inspector's turn to sit and wonder what could be done. He was glad it wasn't his decision. Any search would have to wait until daybreak, and if the girls really had been abducted, they could already be miles away. He sighed audibly.

Ten minutes later, his telephone rang, and he quickly picked up the receiver. To his surprise, it was the Chief Constable himself rather than Superintendent Waller.

"Hardy here, Inspector. I'm going to ask Scotland Yard for help. Hopefully, they'll be able to send detectives. But I want you to organise searching parties ready to start in the morning. Every available constable and sergeant including those in the CID, specials, anyone you can find. Civilians, even – put anyone like that with a police officer."

"Yes, sir. Where should they search?"

"The school buildings and grounds for a start. There aren't many houses within half a mile of the place, but there are farms around. Get people to call on those. This is going to take some organising. I appreciate you want to get off home, but I know I can rely on you. Waller is coming back to your station too – he's going to arrange publicity, press notices, radio announcements, and so on. I gather you have an officer in the school at present – nothing he can do there tonight. Explain to him what we're doing, and tell him to pass that on to Lucy Armstrong. Then he can come back and help you. All understood?"

"Yes, sir."

Hatrick let out another expletive as Colonel Hardy ended the call. He then jiggled the receiver rest, and when he got through to the operator he asked for Willowbank School. As he anticipated, he was told the line was busy, but he instructed the operator to cut into the call.

A few minutes later he found himself speaking to the Headmistress herself, and so he passed on the Chief Constable's message. Miss Armstrong professed herself satisfied, and undertook to send Sergeant Ellis back to the police station.

Hatrick knew that the Super kept a set of detailed maps of the area in his office, and went to find them. The Ordnance Survey 'Six-inch' map sheets were contained in a huge binder, which the Inspector picked up to take back to his own office. As he passed the Desk Sergeant he paused and asked the man to check if there were any CID officers around. Seconds later, he learned that Detective Sergeant Lacey was in the building.

"Tell him to come to my office right away," instructed Hatrick. "When you've done that, I need to organise search parties for first thing in the morning."

He explained the position briefly. "Get hold of every officer we have who isn't at death's door, and have him here in the station by half past seven in the morning. I want civilians too – see if you and your colleagues can think of a dozen or so responsible men to join us."

Hatrick moved off lugging the big folder. He had just set this down on a table in his office and opened it to show the sheet covering Willowbank, when Lacey arrived.

"Where is Mr Frobisher?" enquired Hatrick.

It seemed that the Detective Inspector was away for a few days, visiting his aged mother over a hundred miles away. Lacey was, *pro tem*, the senior CID man.

"Unusual situation, Sergeant. On the direct authority of the Chief Constable, I'm conscripting you for a case."

It took only a minute to explain the salient points to the DS, who whistled as Hatrick concluded.

"I can get our three DCs in for the search, sir. What should we do?"

"Well, it seems to have fallen to me to organise this. I have no idea of the size of this place, but I imagine it's extensive. I'm told there are eight separate boarding houses, for a start, and I guess there will be outbuildings. So let's say the four of you are responsible for searching the school. I'm also authorised to make use of civilians where necessary. Do you reckon you could find four reputable men – friends or in-laws or something – who you could sort of deputise?

"I think so, yes."

All right. Find some, and put each man with one of your chaps. That'll give us four search parties, each containing a police officer. Each of them can take two of the houses. Frankly, I have no idea how long it'll take to go through each one, but it must be done thoroughly. When those are done, the searchers move into the main school. You'll have to defer decisions about who goes where in the main building until you get there in the morning and get an idea of what the search will entail. I'll be there as well, and we'll liaise with the senior staff.

"It gets light enough by about eight o'clock, so we should aim to be on site at ten minutes to.

"I've got the six-inch maps here, and I'm going to divide up the grounds and the nearby areas into however many search parties I can muster. But I can't help feeling that this is a stable door job. If these children really have been kidnapped, it's very unlikely that they'll be within searching range."

There was a tap on the door, and Ellis came in.

"I'm back, sir. Nothing further to report." He grinned at his fellow-sergeant, who was a close friend.

"Pleased to see Mr Hatrick has found some work for you plain-clothes men, Jim!"

"Today we can find work for almost anyone, Ellis – even a 'gentleman of the road' could assist with this search," rebuked the Inspector. "But CID officers are especially valuable, so this isn't the time to joke about them."

He relayed what the Chief Constable had decreed.

"What are they doing up at the school?"

"I don't think they're doing anything after the initial search, sir. They seem to have locked up all the girls – other than a prefect who was helping a teacher with searching, I never saw a single one. The only staff I met were the Secretary, the Bursar, and the Deputy Head, and they were all standing around looking harassed. Miss Armstrong must be under an awful lot of pressure, but even after she'd broken the news to the second parent she still seemed icy calm."

The Inspector grunted.

"She must have been feeling harassed under the mask, Ellis. Anyway, your first job is to help Everett downstairs with contacting our men about coming in tomorrow even if they aren't supposed to be on duty. You'll have to send men around to homes to let people know. And we're also looking for some civilian volunteers."

"I'm sure my brother and brother-in-law would both come in, sir. I'll fix that."

"Good. One other thing. God knows how many men we can recruit, but we need to get them to Willowbank, and we have nowhere near enough cars. Get onto Aldis, and see if he can supply one of his buses – maybe we'll need two. To be here by seven-thirty in the morning. Got all that? You two carry on, then."

Hatrick returned to the map. As Colonel Hardy had said, there were very few houses near to the school, and most of these were tied cottages associated with farms. He pencilled a circle on the relevant map, centred on the school and with a radius of about one mile. He then made a note of the name of each of the farms within the circle. Having done that he let out a sigh. He was still bending over the map when Superintendent Waller entered the room.

"Update, please," requested the Super. Hatrick gave an outline of what he was arranging, including the buses.

"Good. Well done. I was pleased the Chief authorised us to press civilians in for this exercise. We don't have enough men of our own.

"I see you're doing well here, so I'll leave you to get on with everything. I have to arrange for radio broadcasts and local newspapers. I'll need the loudspeaker car to go round the district in the morning, so don't earmark that car for anything else. I'll draft some wording for the driver to use.

"Apparently the parents of those missing have now been contacted, and have already agreed to supply photographs of the children to the national dailies. So that's in hand. If these children turn up following some sort of escapade, they are going to suffer much embarrassment, and hopefully a lot worse. Right, carry on. I'll come back and see you again in half an hour or so. But before I forget, make sure you get a few hours' sleep tonight – and you'd better take charge on site in the morning. Even if the Yard sends detectives, they'll not want to be involved in the search. God knows what they will do, in fact – unless or until some ransom demand arrives."

The Super left the room, and Hatrick returned to his planning.

CHAPTER 3

In New Scotland Yard, things were happening. When the first call had come in from one of the influential parents, the Commissioner of Police had just arrived home. The incoming call had rapidly been routed to the most senior officer still in the building. This happened to be a uniformed Superintendent, who normally dealt with traffic and transport. Recognising the potential importance of the call, Superintendent Brough took it on himself to obtain the Commissioner's home telephone number, and bypassing the intermediate ranks, called the supremo, Sir Philip Game, directly. While actually speaking to the Commissioner (something he had never done before), an officer passed him a written message from another very important person, and after quickly scanning this the Superintendent passed the gist of this on to Sir Philip too.

The Commissioner also recognised the potential eruption this situation was likely to produce.

"Very well, Brough. Quite right to call me.

Find the most senior officer on the crime side that you can – try the AC(C) first, and work downwards if you have to. Say from me that I want a team of first-class detectives down at Willowbank School first thing in the morning. Then get onto the Chief Constable of Kent – I assume he is already aware of this – and tell him that the powers-that-be are asking for the Yard to be involved. Technically we need the CC to invite us, but I expect he'll do that without much prompting. Keep me informed of any developments, until you can hand over to a CID officer. Sorry you've had to be involved."

Brough had hardly replaced the receiver when another incoming call was routed to him, and he found himself speaking to Colonel Hardy, who started off by immediately asking for assistance. Brough passed on the Commissioner's edict, and the Chief Constable was clearly pleased. Hardy gave the Superintendent more details than had already reached the Yard, and Brough said he would ensure that all this would be passed to whichever detective was appointed.

By nine o'clock in the evening, it had been decided that Detective Chief Inspector David Adair would be sent to investigate, supported by three other detectives – Inspector Barry Davison and Sergeants James Borthwick and Patrick Gemmill.

DCI Adair was just thirty-eight years old. He had been in his present rank for four years, which meant he had been promoted very young. He was a little under average height for a policeman, and rather on the tubby side with light, almost blonde, hair. He may not have looked like a classic hero, but he possessed one of the most astute brains in the Met. He was tipped to fill the next vacancy for Superintendent.

Davison was only a year or so younger than his leader, but physically quite different, being six foot five and built like a beanpole. He had jet black hair, and normally wore spectacles. He had worked with Adair for three years, and the two men got on well.

The Sergeants might almost have been twins. They were short, tough, nuggety men, both thirty years of age. Had anyone seen them in certain parts of the country – in South Wales or Nottinghamshire, for example – it would immediately have been assumed that they were coal miners dressed for a day off. Each had great respect for the two senior officers, with whom they had been working for over a year. They were also friends, and had known each other since joining the Met on the same day in 1926.

Adair was at home when his instructions arrived. His subordinates were all still out on other cases, and he had to wait until nearly ten o'clock before being able to pass on his order – "be at the Yard ready for an 'away' case by seven-thirty" – to the last one. None of the four men was happy at being diverted from the pile of cases he was already involved with.

However, each carrying a small suitcase, the

three junior officers all arrived at New Scotland Yard almost simultaneously just before half past seven, and walked upstairs to the DCI's office. Adair, who had come in ten minutes earlier to find a pile of messages on his desk, waved his colleagues towards chairs without looking up from his reading. The three sat in silence while their boss finished perusing the papers. A few minutes later he looked up.

"'Morning, gentlemen. I'm not quite sure what to make of this job. But it's very clear that it has the potential to be front page in the newspapers, get questions in Parliament, and have interference from every Tom, Dick and Harry who has power and influence in the land. So."

He passed on such information as he had. Overnight, another eight messages had been received from important people – none added anything useful to the limited amount of information, but each one served to emphasise the political importance of the case. Adair noted the fact that neither of the relevant fathers had made contact to apply pressure. Not yet, anyway.

"The local lads are starting a search of the school and surrounding area as we speak. We won't be getting involved in that – our task is to act as detectives. Frankly, I have no idea what we can do as yet, but don't pass that thought to anyone outside this room!

"We'd better take two cars. Davison, you and Borthwick go in one; Gemmill, you come with me.

Shouldn't take above an hour to get there. Let's go."

Adair's time estimate was good, and at twenty minutes to nine Gemmill swung his car past the lodges flanking the Willowbank gates, and started up the long drive. He pulled up close to what was clearly the main entrance. As the two men got out, the second car drew up beside them. The four detectives moved to the door, and Borthwick pulled the bell handle.

As for Ellis the previous evening, the door opened almost immediately, but this time by someone who was evidently a maid.

"Are you the London policemen?" she asked.

Adair agreed that they were.

"My orders are to show you into the room where a local policeman is organising the search parties," announced the girl, who looked as though she wasn't long out of school herself. "Then I'm to go and inform Miss Armstrong that you're here, and she'll come and see you."

The detectives were led only a few yards along a corridor, and shown into a room which might have been the waiting room for a doctor, dentist, or solicitor. The central table though, rather than having magazines on it, was covered with map sheets and notepads. Inspector Hatrick was standing beside the table talking to two people in civilian clothes. He came to attention as he saw the Yard officers enter.

"No, you carry on, Inspector," said Adair, "we'll wait."

Hatrick had already noted the report from the two men.

"All right. As you've finished your two houses first, you can start on the school. Take what they call the 'west extension'. Here's a simple sketch map the Secretary has given me. Carry on."

The Inspector turned back to the newcomers. He correctly identified Adair as being the senior.

"Welcome to Willowbank, sir. My name is Hatrick, and for my sins I've been given the job of searching the school and the surrounding area."

Adair shook hands, and introduced himself and his colleagues.

"There are what seem to be toilet facilities for visitors through the next door along the corridor, should you need them, gentlemen," the Inspector helpfully informed his new colleagues.

All four detectives thought they would pay a visit.

"How are you getting on?" enquired the DCI, on returning a few minutes later.

"We've roped in a load of civilians to help, sir – that last pair was a DC with the friend of another officer. I've got twenty-five pairs out there at the moment – some in the school, some combing the grounds, and some doing the rounds of local farms and cottages.

"In fact the Headmistress organised a search of the boarding houses and the main school last night, so it's unlikely that my men will have any joy on the premises. But we obviously have to do it again, and thoroughly.

"I assume you've been given details of the missing children, sir?"

"I have their names, ages, rough descriptions, and a great deal of information about the affluence – and influence – of their relatives. What else do you know?"

"Not much, to be honest. They weren't in the same class, nor in the same boarding house. There seems to be no reason why they would associate together after school. If, as the Head seems to be assuming, these girls have been kidnapped, there's no mystery as to why they were selected. What is a complete mystery is how they were abducted, presumably both pretty much at the same time."

Adair was about to reply when the young maid returned.

"Miss Armstrong would like the London policemen to join her in her office," she reported.

The girl led the four detectives along to the Head's room. She tapped on the door, opened it without waiting, and stood aside.

The Yard officers saw three women and a man seated at the large table to the side of the enormous room. All rose as the officers entered.

Adair introduced himself and his colleagues, and Miss Armstrong did the same for herself and her staff. There was much handshaking.

"Come and sit down, gentlemen – we can

all squeeze in around the table. You've come a fair way, let's get you some refreshments. We've just had some. Angela, please rustle up coffee and biscuits for our visitors."

The Secretary, who looked very nervous, left the room without speaking, and everyone else sat down.

Although Adair hadn't heard the discussion between Hatrick and Ellis the previous evening, he would have recognised the description of the senior staff. The Deputy Head, Mrs Livermore, and the Bursar, Mr Dodds, both looked distraught. Miss Armstrong, however, might have been entertaining potential parents, or attending a routine staff meeting.

"Let's get on, Chief Inspector. Thank you for coming, although I imagine pressure was brought to bear to get your involvement. I'm not sure what you have been told, so let me just give you an outline."

The Head gave an efficient précis of the situation. She ended by emphasising that both girls enjoyed life in the school, and both excelled in lessons and in games.

"Put another way, neither Megan nor Aaliyah had any reason to run away.

"Although my staff conducted a search of the school last night, your local colleagues are doing so again this morning, as of course they should. I understand that the search area is also being extended outside the grounds.

"I assume you will want to interview the girls in the two relevant classes, and also those in the missing girls' houses?"

"That's right, ma'am. Also members of your staff – teachers, maids, other ancillary staff like cooks, groundsmen, and so on."

"Yes, of course. You'll need a room – and no doubt a telephone would be useful. You'd better have my Secretary's office next door. Bill – Angela will have to move in with you *pro tem*." The Bursar nodded at once.

Adair thought to himself that although Christian names were used among this senior group, it was pretty clear that it was not a democracy – what the Head said would be accepted without question.

"I'd like you to let me have a list of all the children, especially noting which ones were in the missing girl's houses, and in their year," said the DCI. "And another list of all the staff of whatever grade. Also details of any visitors who might have been present at any time yesterday – and that would include delivery drivers and the like."

"Understood," replied the Head. "I'll get Angela to organise those things as soon as she returns."

As she spoke, the Secretary returned carrying a large jug in one hand and a smaller milk jug in the other. She was followed by another maid bearing a tray with cups and saucers, and a sugar bowl.

While the coffee was being poured, Adair looked around the room and out of the window. He guessed that this room would have been the dining room of the original house. The décor – particularly the ceiling plasterwork was exquisite. The wings built on each side of the house, and the extensions on the back of each of those, narrowed the angle of view down to a lake, but the vista was still beautiful.

The DCI brought his attention back to business, as Miss Armstrong gave Angela Spencer her instructions.

"No problem, Lucy. I'll move my typewriter and a few other files and things into your room now, Bill. And I'll have the lists ready for you within ten or fifteen minutes, Chief Inspector."

"Good. Now, how do you want to play this, Chief Inspector? Presumably you'll want to talk to the girls in the two relevant classes first, and the two teachers – both happen to be residents. Would you like us to organise those for you – get them to queue up outside your room?"

"It would certainly be good to start with those two groups – thank you. First, the two teachers separately, in the office. However, at this stage I don't think it's necessary to see each pupil individually. Perhaps the two classes could be in their respective classrooms, and we'll see them there. I'd estimate a quarter of an hour for each.

"After that, we will split into two interviewing pairs, and we'll need to speak to every member of staff, and each child in the two relevant houses. If every half-hour or so we give Miss Spencer a list of the people we'd like to see next, someone – perhaps one of your maids – could be given the job of finding them and bringing them to our room."

"Yes, that's straightforward. All the girls are currently confined to their houses, and those in the two relevant classes are probably spread across all eight houses. It'll take us half an hour to extract all those girls and get them into the classrooms.

"Eleanor, start getting that arranged, please – use prefects to take messages from house to house. Get the girls assembled in the actual classrooms they were in last thing yesterday – let's make it as realistic as possible.

"Angela, please find Pat and Danielle. Get one of them to report to your office straight away, and the other to come in about fifteen minutes. Tell them we're collecting their classes, but they don't need to be present while the Chief Inspector is seeing their girls – indeed, I imagine he would prefer not to have an authoritarian presence which might deter some child from speaking out.

"Happy, Chief Inspector?"

"Yes indeed, ma'am."

"Right, off you go, ladies. Eleanor, come and tell the officers when the classes have been assembled, and show him where to go."

"While you're finding Pat, Angela, I'll move your typewriter into my office," said the Bursar.

The three staff members all left the room to carry out their instructions.

"Go through to next door, gentlemen," said Adair, "I just want a quick word with the Headmistress."

When the connecting door closed behind his men, Adair looked at Miss Armstrong. She spoke first.

"Before you say or ask whatever you want to, I have a question. In your experience, how long is it likely to be before we hear from the kidnappers? I assume now that we are facing that situation.

"Unfortunately, I don't have any such experience. I don't even recall a case within the Met. But I've read about one or two cases elsewhere, and I think the ransom demand might arrive within a day or so."

"Yes. Well, I'm not stupid, and I am horribly aware that there have been cases where the kidnapped person is killed – after the demand is issued, the abductor perhaps fearing that the police were getting close."

"I can't deny that possibility, ma'am. Much will depend on how the demand is made. It might be direct to the parents. That could be complicated, as they could decide not to inform the police. Or the demand could come to the school. You would, I imagine, feel obligated to inform the parents before telling us. Or the demand could be made publicly, via a newspaper, for example. But, with respect, I think we should consider that when – or if – such a demand arrives."

"Very well. How can I help now?"

"Just a few things, ma'am. First, the Yard received messages last night and this morning from a dozen or so very influential people. But the parents of the two missing girls were not among them. Can you tell me how they took this?"

"I spoke to both fathers. They were shocked, as you would expect. But both, although angry, remained calm. Aaliyah's father, Yussef Hammadani, is always inscrutable, and in fact I imagine he rarely ever loses his composure. But if you were to find the culprit, and then left him alone in a room with Mr Hammadani, I rather think only one man would come out alive.

"Megan's father has the archetypal stiff upper lip, as one would perhaps expect in the 12th holder of an English earldom. But put in the same room as the kidnapper, I think it likely that he would behave in the same way as Mr Hammadani – although he wouldn't benefit from the diplomatic immunity that I understand Mr H enjoys."

"What about your other parents – what's been the general reaction?"

"Mixed. Four girls have been removed from the school. All, I am assured, will eventually return. Most parents, on being assured that adequate steps are being taken to ensure that the girls will be kept in until the matter is cleared up, have been content to allow their children to remain."

"Good. Now another question – a matter of curiosity, really. I was surprised to see you have a male among your senior staff. Does Mr Dodds live on the school premises?"

"He doesn't as it happens. Bill lives four or five miles away, and comes in every day. But we do have other males, Chief Inspector, and all those do reside here.

"Brian and Cerys Redpath are married. Both are teachers here – Brian is the only male teacher – and although Cerys is nominally one of the housemistresses, in practice they share the job.

"Then we have April and Jonathan Harvey. April, who as Miss Ross was unmarried until a few months ago, has been a housemistress here for several years. Then, she married Jonathan – a very personable man. He doesn't work – I understand he has private means. I believe he also helps April to run her house.

"I can see you're wondering why I only 'believe' and 'understand' – well that's because this is my first term here, and I've only met him a few times.

"Then we have Eleanor Livermore. Although Deputy Head, she is also a housemistress. She lives – or lived – with her husband in Somerville House. Keith Livermore is the school doctor. I don't mean he is an employee – he is a local GP with a practice in town. The staff and the children here are all his private patients – the school pays the fees for the non-teaching staff, although referrals to the doctor have been very few. Keith met Eleanor here, and they married a year or two ago, I understand. However, only the day before yesterday she reported to me that they are, temporarily at least, separated, and he has moved out. I haven't mentioned that to another soul as yet, and so I don't know how widely it is known among staff or pupils. Again, I imagine that the Doctor helped in the House.

"But neither Megan nor Aaliyah are in any of those three houses.

"We also have two male groundsmen. One, Painter, is married – his wife is a cook in Burdett-Coutts House. They live in one of the lodges at the front gate. The other, Green, is a bachelor. He lives in the other lodge. I suppose you might call the lodges 'tied cottages'.

There is a porter, odd-job man, general factotum if you like. His name is Bailey, and he must be over fifty. He has a room on the top floor of this building. Five of our maids, who work in the old house and the main school, also have rooms in here. Each of the six is allocated to a particular house for meals.

"I also have a set of rooms immediately above this one. I can make my own breakfast, and I hardly eat at lunchtime, but I usually take my evening meal in one of the houses – there is a sort of rota.

"Finally, we have another male odd-job man, Dalby. He's over sixty, and apart from war service has apparently worked here since 1897. He is a widower, and lives in one of the lodges by the rear entrance. The other rear lodge is currently unoccupied.

"You're thinking of having men around a lot of girls. And it's true that many of our older ones are undeniably attractive young women. Well, we've never had a problem here. My predecessor told me she kept a wary eye on Green – he's about twenty-five and the only one who might conceivably be attractive to a girl of eighteen or so – for the first few months he was here, and she said she was very happy that he knows how to behave. When I took over, I asked other staff to comment as well, and everyone said the same thing. Actually I suppose it's even possible that he is homosexual – I've never heard of a girlfriend."

"Thanks. Now, a crucial point. The girls were last seen at about four o'clock, and were found to be missing at six-thirty. If they were abducted, it was probably within the first half hour. Obviously, I'll be asking all the adults where they were at that time."

"You're thinking that one of my staff is responsible? I have to accept the possibility, of course. Well, I can provide a few alibis.

"We had a staff meeting in this office at four-fifteen. It lasted until about half past five. With three exceptions, all the teaching staff were present, as was Angela.

"Cerys Redpath had a hospital appointment.

Her husband owns a car, and as Cerys can't drive, Brian took her to the hospital. The other absent teacher was Felicity Townsend, our youngest member of staff. She lives with her mother a few miles away, and also owns a car in which she comes to work each day. She asked if I'd excuse her attendance at the meeting as her mother is apparently poorly. As Cerys's father is dead, and as Mrs Townsend had been on her own all day, I agreed, naturally.

"So with those exceptions – and I refuse to believe any of those three could be involved – the teachers can't be guilty.

"I can also vouch for old Dalby. He was working with two plumbers that we'd had to call in to find and deal with a problem with heating pipes in the main school hall. None of them could have been involved. I saw all three in there at about half past three, and at about ten to seven Dalby came to tell me that they had finished at last."

"Thanks for all that, ma'am; most helpful. I'll get on now. But if you hear anything – whether from a parent or a kidnapper, please inform me immediately."

Adair had stood up, but Miss Armstrong motioned him to wait.

"Have you arranged for somewhere to stay, Chief Inspector?"

"Not as yet, ma'am. We'll sort that out this afternoon."

"It occurs to me that you could stay here –

I imagine that would be more convenient. We do have two suites in the old house where overnight visitors can be accommodated. However, each of the houses has a small sick bay, with a bathroom attached. I understand none is occupied at present. Using those would mean that your men could have one each – and you could take your meals with the girls in that house. There is no problem with that. If you wanted to get together for a drink after the evening meal, you could always drive down to the pub in Davyton village – it doesn't have beds so you can't stay there. All I'd ask is that you return to your respective houses by half past ten. It wouldn't be fair to expect the housemistresses to stay up later to let you in, and even in the case of policemen I really can't have people wandering around at night!"

Adair paused to think. There were advantages and disadvantages to the offer. Eventually, he decided that the former marginally outweighed the latter, and accepted with thanks.

"Perhaps Inspector Davison could be billeted in Lady Megan's house, with me in Aaliyah's. The sergeants can go to whichever houses are convenient."

Miss Armstrong said that would be arranged. As Adair again stood up to go she asked if he was married with children of his own.

"Yes, ma'am, I have a wife, Rebecca, and a six-year-old daughter Sophia. Not yet old enough to come here, of course."

Adair wondered if the question was intended to ascertain the reliability of the policemen around so many children, and immediately added, "the inspector is also married with a son the same age as my daughter. My two sergeants are also married, but not for very long, and neither has children as yet. I'll see you later, ma'am."

He passed through into the Secretary's office, and issued an instruction as soon as he had closed the door behind him.

Borthwick, go and see Inspector Hatrick. Ask him if he is including the four estate lodges by the front and rear gates in the search. It seems three of the four have a male occupier, and the fourth is allegedly unoccupied but could perhaps be used to hold a couple of children. Technically, I suppose we might need a warrant."

"Right. All four of us can be present when the two teachers come in, and we'll all go to the classrooms and see if anything is to be learned there. After that, you take Borthwick, Inspector, and I'll take Gemmill. We'll sort out the list when we get back here, and divide the jobs between us.

"Interesting chat with Miss Armstrong just now – I'll tell you about it when Borthwick comes back."

Adair looked around this office. The view from the window was the same as the Head enjoyed, but here the proportions of the room were all wrong. There was only one window, and the wall on the side away from Miss Armstrong looked decidedly flimsy. He thought that the drawing room of the original mansion would have been located in this position, and guessed – correctly – that it had been divided to create two or three offices. He was still considering this when Borthwick returned.

"All done, sir. The Inspector says that all three occupiers allowed a thorough search without making any objections. And one got the key for the unoccupied lodge, and that was searched too. Apparently it doesn't look as though anyone has set foot in the place for many months."

"Oh well, I knew that possibility was too good to be likely. Right, first point is this. We've all been invited to stay in the school tonight. Each of us will sleep in a house sickbay, and eat with the girls in that house. After we've eaten, separately, we might go down to the local pub. We'll see."

CHAPTER 4

There was a tap on the door, and a woman stuck her head in the room. "I'm Patricia Trelawney," she announced. "Are you ready to talk to me?"

"Yes indeed," said Adair, getting to his feet. "Please come in and take a seat. I'm Chief Inspector Adair, and with me are Inspector Davison, and Sergeants Gemmill and Borthwick.

Mrs Trelawney looked to be in her mid-to-late forties, was of average height and had greying hair. She was wearing a navy-blue skirt, and cream blouse. The spectacles she was wearing suited her face very well, thought Adair.

Everyone sat down, and Mrs Trelawney looked expectantly at the DCI.

"We understand Megan was in your last class yesterday afternoon. What was the subject?"

"English grammar. At this school every girl has an hour on that once a week up to the age of fifteen. By that age, and after four years of study, they are deemed to be competent in the subject!"

Adair, whose own school had supported a similar ethos, smiled. The other three wondered how learning about English grammar could possibly require four years. They weren't much the wiser when their boss remarked, "I always struggled to remember the difference between gerunds and gerundives – should have come here, perhaps!"

"Feel free to join one of my classes for some refresher training, Chief Inspector," said the lady, with a faint smile.

"A bit late for me, I fear, Mrs Trelawney, but thank you. Now, I'm sure you would have mentioned anything useful already, but was there anything during this lesson – or indeed at a time before or after – which could help us?"

"Nothing, Chief Inspector. The lesson passed just as usual. All our girls are well above average in brainpower, of course, and Megan is in the top two or three in that class – which has fourteen pupils. I also teach her English Literature, another subject in which she excels. However, she is not in my house, and I don't encounter her during games or anywhere else outside my classes.

"To be honest, I rarely see her around the school, so I can't talk about her interests, or her friends, or anything like that.

"Within the English classes, she is always impeccably polite – although that is hardly exceptional here. I do get the impression – and it's no more than that – that she might be something of a loner. When there are a few spare minutes just before I start the lesson, for example, she doesn't seem to chatter much with her neighbours like most of the other girls do. But I've never seen any sign of unpopularity."

"At the end of that class, four o'clock, I think, did you see what she did?"

"No. Two other girls came up to my desk with questions, and I spent seven or eight minutes with them. By the time we had finished, all the others had disappeared."

"I see, thank you. How long have you taught here, Mrs Trelawney?"

"Eighteen years. I qualified in 1912, and taught at another school for a year before marrying and becoming a housewife. Then the war came. My husband was badly injured in that, and later died of his wounds. That was in 1919. We didn't have children. I applied for a post here, was appointed, and have been here ever since. I became a housemistress about ten years ago.

"I have no doubt you are looking at this being an 'inside job', and certainly I think some information must have come from inside. If this is indeed a kidnapping with intent to extract a ransom, the selection of the children of what are probably two of the richest men in the world doesn't look like coincidence.

"You'll also be suspicious of every male around. I can't criticise you for that. However, my personal view is that the three men here who are the husbands of teachers – and indeed one is a teacher himself – could never have been involved in such a scheme. They are all men of the highest integrity.

"I can't comment on the two groundsmen, or on Bailey or old Dalby, except to say that none of them would have had the information to select those two particular girls."

"If indeed they were selected," remarked Adair.

"*Touché*," replied Mrs Trelawney.

"This looks like a nasty abduction business. But, as your Head has already realised, it could be – or could become – a murder case. I need hardly say that there can be no secrets. Anything – anything at all – which might be relevant must be disclosed. What I'm getting at is this. Do you know of any disgruntled member of staff? Anyone having disagreements with the Head, or difficulties with some children?"

"No, Chief Inspector. This is a particularly happy school, and we are fortunate to be very well led. Or at least, it was a very happy school until yesterday," she added as an afterthought.

Adair thanked the teacher, and the officers all stood as she left the room. As she opened the door, she found a colleague about to knock on it, and turned to speak to the detectives.

"Danny Ovenden is here, gentlemen – can she come in?"

"Certainly, thank you," called the DCI.

Adair went through the introductions as before. This teacher was about the same age as

Mrs Trelawney, slim and fair-haired. All four men independently thought that this lady must have been a real beauty in her youth.

"Is it Miss or Mrs?" enquired Adair.

"Alas, it's Miss, Chief Inspector. My fiancé died at Jutland in 1916. I managed to hook another young man a year later. We had just got engaged, and then he was killed at Cambrai barely a month before the Armistice. I decided that someone up above didn't want me to marry, and so I gave up on the idea. I contemplated entering a nunnery – I was very depressed – but decided I could be more use as a teacher."

"Actually, I would have been totally unsuitable as a nun. I was brought up notionally Catholic, but the war turned me against organised religion. Please don't tell Lucy Armstrong, but I'm now nearer to being an atheist than an agnostic. Sorry, I'm rambling.

"You want to know whether I have any idea about what happened to Aaliyah. The answer is that I don't have a clue. I teach mainly history, although I occasionally help out with English if another teacher is sick. That last lesson yesterday was about the Enclosures – particularly the 'Inclosure Acts' of 1773 and 1845. A number of the girls come from landed families who may well have benefited from enclosures over many years. Curiously it was Aaliyah, with no ancient line of English gentry behind her, who asked the most penetrating questions and perhaps took the greatest interest. A very nice child; I hope no harm has come to her.

"Anyway, the class broke up, and the girls all left the room. I didn't see who went off with whom, or where any of them went. By the time I had gathered up my papers and so on, they had all disappeared. I went to the school library, wanting to consult a book. I didn't see Aaliyah in there.

"I should also say that she is not in my house, and apart from in my history class this year – and last year – I don't see the girl."

"Do you know if she has any particular friends?"

"She sits beside Geraldine Wyatt in class, and they do seem to chatter together, given half a chance. But I can't say whether that is a real friendship or simply that in my class they happen to be neighbours. But Geraldine and Aaliyah are in the same house."

Adair glanced at his colleagues to see if anyone had another question, but three heads were shaken. He thanked Miss Ovenden, and escorted her to the door. The Deputy Head was waiting outside.

"The first class – Megan's – is ready for you, Chief Inspector. If you care to follow me, I'll show you the way."

As the detectives followed Mrs Livermore along the corridor, the DCI gave his colleagues some instructions:

"I'll do the talking, gentlemen. You range

yourselves at the front facing the children. Stand, if necessary. Look for any sign – I have no idea what it might be – that suggests a girl is uncomfortable. Might be an indication that she knows something relevant – or thinks that she might know something relevant – but is afraid to speak for some reason."

The little group reached a door, and the Deputy paused. A buzz of conversation could be heard faintly from inside.

"Do you want me to introduce you, Chief Inspector?"

"Thank you, no. We'll take it from here."

"Very well. In twenty minutes or so, the other class will have assembled. Two doors further along – just go and join the girls. As you requested, each class is in the same room that it was in yesterday afternoon. Please send the girls back to their houses when you've finished."

Mrs Livermore turned to go, and Adair opened the classroom door. The buzz of conversation stopped instantly, and there was the unmistakable schoolroom sound of thirteen children rising to their feet.

"Please sit down, young ladies," said Adair. "Now, I don't know what you have been told, but all four of us are detectives from Scotland Yard in London, here to help find your two colleagues who seem to have disappeared. I am Chief Inspector Adair; the very tall gentleman to your right is Inspector Davison; and to your left are Sergeants

Borthwick and Gemmill. Some of you will be seeing a bit more of at least one of us, as we've been invited to stay overnight in the boarding houses, and eat with you while we're here.

"As we speak, local police officers are searching both inside and outside the school. It is very important that we find Megan and Aaliyah as soon as possible.

"Now, Megan and most of you left this room at four o'clock yesterday afternoon. First of all, who was with her as you actually left the room? We don't know your names, of course, so if you speak please tell us who you are."

There was a short silence. Then a chubby black-haired girl raised her hand diffidently.

"I'm Chloe McCormack, sir. Megan sits next to me in this class." The girl indicated the empty desk beside her. "I was talking to her as we left the classroom. But outside the door we split up – we're in different houses, you see, and our paths were in opposite directions."

"Well that's a good start, Chloe – thanks. What were you talking about.

"Nothing that would suggest what was in her mind, I think, sir – word and phrase modifiers. That's what Mrs T had been teaching us in the lesson. And I hope you won't tell her I said this, but Megan and I were just agreeing that they were the most boring things in grammar we'd ever met."

Around the classroom there was a ripple of what was clearly support for this statement.

Adair smiled. "I couldn't disagree with that. But, as you say, it probably doesn't take us any further. I don't want to put words in your mouth, Chloe, but was Megan's behaviour in any way strange – did she seem excited, for example?"

"Not that I noticed, sir."

"Did she say anything else – for instance did she say 'I'm going straight back to my house' or 'I'm going to the library' or something like that?"

"Sorry – I didn't hear her say anything. We finished the few words about the lesson as we reached the corridor. It was a bit crowded outside the classroom door, and we split up. I went to the right. Megan would have gone to the left – that's the shortest way to her house – but I didn't actually see her go."

A blonde girl put up her hand. "My name is Petra Andrews, sir. Megan did turn left out of the classroom, sir. I saw her. She was walking along a few feet ahead of me. But at the next junction in the corridor, I turned off again and she was still going straight ahead."

Thank you, Petra. At the point you turned off, was anyone with Megan?"

"Definitely not, sir. But here's the thing. I didn't think anything of this at the time, but, now you've asked, it does seem odd. She and I are in the same house. I was going back there. The way she was walking isn't the quickest way."

"Useful information," the DCI said, thoughtfully. "The way she was going, Petra –

where might that lead to?"

The girl considered the question for a moment.

"Well, it doesn't go to anywhere else in the school, sir. A few yards further along at the end of that corridor is just an external door. You might use that way out if you were going to the swimming pool. Or if you were just going out for a walk in the grounds – although that isn't the usual way out to the park."

A number of girls nodded in agreement.

"But the swimming pool isn't open at that time," Petra added, "and it's very unlikely anyone would be going for a walk after nightfall."

"No, I see. Thank you Petra. Would you call yourself a close friend of Megan?"

Again, the girl considered her answer.

"We get along all right," she replied. "I see and talk to her every day, of course, as we're in the same house and mostly in the same class. But we don't sort of do everything together. In the school we have what I suppose could be called little cliques, and I'm not in hers. I guess you are wondering if Meg said anything earlier about what she intended to do. Well, she and I are on perfectly good terms, but I'm not her confidante."

Adair thought that last sentence could have been uttered by an adult, and he smiled to himself.

"Fair enough. These little cliques. Might one contain members from different houses?"

"Oh yes," replied Petra, and several other

girls nodded.

"Is there anyone among you who you might call herself in a clique with Megan – a confidante even?"

Nobody spoke for several seconds, and then there was a loud whisper. "Come on, Lotty, you and Meg are as close as can be."

With evident reluctance, a girl raised her hand.

"I suppose I am, sir. My name is Charlotte Wickham. We're in the same house, and we've been friends since we arrived here three years ago. But I honestly don't know where she is. And it seems awful to say anything about her when she isn't here."

All the detectives stared at her. After a moment, the DCI spoke quietly.

"Two girls are missing. They have not been found after an extensive search of the school. Your Headmistress tells me that there is no reason for them to run away.

"The inescapable conclusion is that they didn't leave the premises of their own free will. If that is the case it probably means that they have been abducted. There will be a ransom demand for their safe return, most likely. I hadn't intended to spell this out – in fact I assumed that at your age you would work out the situation for yourselves. But, to put it very bluntly, their lives are in danger. It is not unknown for kidnap victims to be murdered – even if a ransom is paid.

"So please don't think that it's sneaking to inform us about any detail which would normally be kept secret. That would be plain silly – and I'm sure you can all see that it wouldn't be in Megan's interest.

"For example, just now I told you what Miss Armstrong told me – that neither girl had any reason to run away. Now as the two of them were apparently not close, it doesn't seem likely that they would have run away together. Nevertheless, if any of you even thinks that there may be a reason for their doing so, speak now."

He paused for a few seconds, his gaze passing over the thirteen faces in front of him, before returning to the 'friend'.

"All right. Now, Charlotte, tell us about Megan's behaviour – her manner if you like – today."

Charlotte brushed a tear from her eye.

"Yes, I'm sorry, sir. I was being stupid. But I really don't know where she went. All I can say is that after lunch she seemed extra happy. I don't mean she isn't normally a happy person, but she seemed...is euphoric a word?"

"It certainly is, Charlotte. Did you see anything that might have caused this euphoria?"

"No. I hadn't spoken to her since breakfast, and as far as I remember she was perfectly normal then. We had different classes during the morning, and then back at the house I wasn't sitting close to her at the lunch table. I was walking back to school with her when I noticed the change.

"I said something like 'you're happy about something', and she just laughed, and said something about looking forward to a treat. I just assumed that maybe a parent or her favourite uncle or godfather or someone was coming to take her out to tea at the weekend.

"But now I don't know. If I'd asked more questions, perhaps she'd still be here." She started to cry openly. The girl on one side of Charlotte put an arm around her, and the one on the other side produced a handkerchief.

"All right, Charlotte," said Adair. "I don't think asking Megan any more questions would have changed anything. Actually, I suspect that she wouldn't have answered you anyway. You bear absolutely no responsibility."

Angela McCormack raised her hand again. "I can confirm what Lotty said about Megan being excited, sir. I noticed earlier in the afternoon that she was sort of bubbling. Didn't stop her concentrating on the work, though – as I said before, she was taking everything in as usual even if some of it was boring."

"Good; thanks again. Now, did anyone see an adult – any adult – talking to Megan between breakfast and lunch?"

There was a general shaking of heads.

"Has anyone else got any more information?

"No? Well, if anything comes to mind, however insignificant it might seem, find one of us at once. Thank you everyone; now go straight back to your houses please."

The girls trooped out, and burst into conversation as soon as they reached the corridor.

Adair looked at his colleagues. "Any sign of anyone looking as though she knew something?" The three detectives shook their heads.

"Are you thinking what I'm thinking, sir?" asked Inspector Davidson. "That someone here promised Megan something really special that afternoon or evening, and swore the girl to secrecy?"

"Exactly that, yes. And Aaliyah too. Anyway, let's go and see the other class.

The buzz of conversation in the other classroom died away as the officers walked in and the fifteen girls here also stood up.

For the next few minutes, this meeting progressed exactly like the previous one. Nobody had seen where Aaliyah had gone on leaving the room at the end of the lesson.

Two girls admitted to being close friends with Aaliyah – both were in her house as well as in this and most of her other classes.

One, who gave her name as Phoebe Brent-Williams, said she had been with Aaliyah at breakfast, and for some of the morning, and had sat next to her at lunch."

The DCI waited, but Phoebe had evidently finished.

"Would you say Aaliyah's mood was

different in any way yesterday – or did you see any change in mood between say breakfast and the last lesson in the afternoon?"

"I didn't notice. She was her usual chatty self."

Adair decided that a leading question was justified, and put it.

"Did you – did any of you – think Aaliyah was particularly happy or excited yesterday?"

The other friend, Geraldine Wyatt, put up her hand again. "Now you mention it, sir, perhaps she did change a bit. During the morning break, she went off somewhere – to the lavatory, I suppose. When I saw her next, as we went into the next lesson, she was certainly smiling. But whether that was a real change or whether I'm just imagining it after you put the thought into my head, I can't honestly say."

"Did anyone accompany Aaliyah when she went to the lavatory during that break?"

Fifteen heads shook.

The DCI made the same point about the danger the girls might now be in, but no further information was gleaned.

After he sent the class out, he looked at his colleagues with raised eyebrows.

They all shook their heads.

"If the theory about the 'treat' is right, sir, perhaps the contact was made during the morning break," suggested Gemmill. "That should narrow down the possibilities."

"Yes; but while the theory is tenable, we really have no idea whether it's correct. Later, over in the boarding houses, we must make a point of asking as many girls in Megan's class as possible if they saw her speak to anyone – an adult, I mean – outside the classroom during the morning.

"In fact, we still don't know for a certainty if this is kidnapping, although that certainly has to be the odds-on favourite.

"But is it feasible that someone – or perhaps two people – could approach highly intelligent girls and promise some obviously attractive treat, and could absolutely guarantee that neither would leak the details to friends?

"Think about that, as we go back to the office."

CHAPTER 5

Back in the office, Adair found that the Secretary had provided the information he had requested. He quickly scanned the papers.

"There are seven year-groups, with an average of about forty girls in each," he read aloud. "A total of two hundred and seventy-seven children. All are boarders, spread over the eight houses. Each house has girls in all the age groups, and there is an explanatory note here saying that rather than having all thirty-five or so children in a house of the same age, each house is designed to be more like a family home, with older and younger siblings.

"The Head has an apartment here in the original building. So do several maids and a porter. Each house has two adults in residence – a housemistress and a house tutor – but each of the three houses in which the housemistress is married has three adults.

"That's seventeen teachers living over the shop, as it were, plus two more husbands." The DCI briefly explained about the Doctor. "A further twelve teachers don't live in – some of them only work part-time.

"Two groundsmen, one odd-job man, one porter, eight cooks, and forty-one maids also live in. Most of the females in the boarding houses, and the males – apart from the one in this building – in the gate lodges.

"Miss Spencer has provided a list of yesterday's visitors, but she has added a *caveat* – she says she can't guarantee that the list is complete. It includes two plumbers – I'll come back to them in a minute – plus various suppliers like the butcher, baker, milkman, and so on, and two pairs of prospective parents who came for a look around and a meeting with the Head.

"Comments so far?"

"Not really relevant, sir," said Gemmill, "but I was struck by the situation of the two teachers we saw – both here really only because of the war."

"Yes; it's very sad, and probably several other members of staff – maybe including the Head herself – will be in the same sort of situation. We have to remember that very few women were killed in the war. A few died in bombing raids, and rather more were killed in one of the various explosions in munitions factories – an awful one at Chilwell, for example. But those numbers were totally insignificant compared to the hundreds of thousands of British men killed. A huge number of women were either widowed, or had their chances of marrying effectively removed.

"As for that being relevant, one never knows

– it could be.

"Getting back to the plumbers. I learned from the Head that almost all the teachers were present at a staff meeting between four-fifteen and five-thirty. As the girls must have been abducted within a few minutes of four o'clock, it looks as though those at the meeting are in the clear. The two plumbers, plus Dalby the maintenance man, are also accounted for. We'll need to see the three teachers who weren't at the meeting, of course, plus the two non-teacher husbands. And all the other members of staff, although I really can't see a kitchen maid being involved.

"Now, there's another note here, written by the Deputy Head. It allocates each of us to a particular house. Lunch is at half-past twelve, and at twelve-ten four prefects will arrive here to escort us to our respective houses. It is suggested that we take our bags at the same time.

"You should all look at the lists to see the name of your house, the names of the staff there, and the names of the children.

"Mr Davison and I will be in the houses where Megan and Aaliyah reside – he is in Wollstonecraft and I'm in Lovelace, but you two sergeants should also take every opportunity to speak to the girls – especially those who are in the same year as the missing two. The list here will tell you who they are – better note them in your pocketbooks.

"In fact, I'm going to change my mind.

Instead of splitting into pairs for interviewing, all four of us will interview the girls – and the teachers – in our respective houses by ourselves.

"Borthwick, I noticed a bus stop just by the entrance gates. When you've finished your house take the car and go and find the offices of the local bus company. Ask for details of the buses passing this point in both directions between four and five thirty yesterday afternoon. Track down the drivers and conductors. If they are out and about, as they probably will be, find out where their buses are going and chase them down. If you're lucky you'll just have to sit by the bus stop here and flag each bus down. Ask the relevant conductors if any girls boarded their bus by the school gates yesterday. I don't think that they did, but we must check.

"That leaves the other four houses, and we'll have to sort out who is going to cover what. Are you all happy about the sort of questions to ask?"

All three detectives nodded.

"Right. Now whoever gets the house with Mr & Mrs Redpath must interview them very thoroughly. They were two of those who missed the staff meeting. The third teacher who wasn't present doesn't live in the school – I'll arrange to see her myself sometime.

"I suggest we aim to meet in this room again at half past four, whether we've finished or not. You may take longer, Borthwick. Then we'll make arrangements for the remaining adults.

"It's too late to start interviews before lunch. I'm going to see how Mr Hatrick is getting on."

***

Adair found the Inspector sitting in a chair with his feet up on the table, and his eyes closed. Evidently he wasn't actually asleep, because although the DCI made no particular noise, as soon as he was through the open door Hatrick jumped to his feet.

"Apologies, sir – I only had a couple of hours sleep last night. Just taking advantage of a lull."

"Understandable, Inspector. Any news?"

"The school itself has been thoroughly checked, as have all the boarding houses. We've been in all four lodges, as I told your sergeant earlier. We've even been in the Headmistress's apartments – very extensive and luxurious, I'm told. We've searched the chapel too. No sign of missing children anywhere.

"The grounds are extensive, but although there are quite a few trees there is actually very little ground cover. Much of it is hockey pitches and the like.

Basically, sir, I'm satisfied that the girls are not within the perimeter of this place. The search teams are all now outside the grounds. We're currently going over the fields and through the woods within a radius of a mile. We're visiting all the various farms and cottages within a radius of two miles – there aren't that many, actually.

"We don't have search warrants, of course, but my men have been instructed to ask for consent to search every barn, byre, stable, pigsty and the like. Also, to look very carefully at everyone they see for signs of guilt – but you'll know yourself that is far easier said than done."

"Too true," replied Adair. "Well, thanks for the update.

"Now, I'm sure you're clear enough about this already, Inspector, but I'll make the point. Although I'm now in charge of this case, your search was ordered before I was given the job, and it isn't part of my remit. I can't order you to stop, nor can I order you to extend the search area – although I could ask your Chief to do so.

"My thinking is this. If these girls have been abducted – and I have to admit that's looking more and more likely – they'll have been taken way outside your search area before the police even got called in. But, as you said to me when I first saw you, this has to be done. So my unofficial suggestion to you is to wind down your search as soon as your men have covered the area you have just indicated."

"Thanks for that, sir. My view is exactly the same as yours. However, the Chief Constable's granddaughter is a pupil at this school, as I expect you've been told. He may well want something more."

"Very probably. Well you'll have to obey orders, of course. But you're very welcome to quote my view to your Chief if it helps."

"One other thing, sir. A couple of newspapermen got to the school earlier. I happened to be by the front door, and sent them packing. I've now stationed a constable on both the entrance gates, with instructions not to let any reporters through. We'll keep the gates guarded for as long as necessary. The Headmistress is aware – and she certainly doesn't want to be bothered by anyone like that."

"Well done. Right – I'm off to eat with a load of chattering girls in a boarding house – what are you doing for food?"

"Oh, the Headmistress has been very good, sir. She's arranged for a meal to be brought to me in here at about half past twelve. She offered to have sandwiches made for the men searching the school and grounds, but since we finished on the premises I decided to bus them down to the Lion and Lamb, and take whatever the publican could rustle up."

"Good. If you are allowed to stop, perhaps you'll just come and tell me – I'll either be in the Secretary's office or in Lovelace House."

The DCI returned to Miss Spencer's office. He was just about to open the door when four girls, all about seventeen years old, materialised beside him. They were not in school uniform, although their outfits weren't really that different – plaid skirts and 'sensible' shoes, but cardigans rather than blazers.

"Are you Chief Inspector Adair, sir?" enquired one.

The DCI admitted that he was.

"I'm Arabella Fairfax, sir, head prefect. My colleagues and I are to escort you and your colleagues to the houses."

"Excellent, thank you. Come in and meet the others."

Inside the office, Arabella, who like the other three was more like a young woman than a schoolgirl, spoke first.

"Our instructions are that you, Chief Inspector, are to be taken to Lovelace – that'll be with Alice Prendergast here. Inspector Davison goes to Wollstonecraft with Pamela Thorndyke. Sergeant Gemmill is in Somerville with Esther Verney. Sergeant Borthwick comes to Burnett-Coutts with me. We are four of the eight school prefects, by the way – each house has one, plus one or two house prefects, who rank slightly lower in the hierarchy.

"After you've each finished talking to the members of your respective houses, sometime this afternoon, I understand that we're to show each of you to another house. Does all that sound acceptable, sir?"

"Perfect; thank you Arabella. Just one irrelevant question. Are school prefects exempt from the uniform requirements?"

The girls all laughed. "We wish it were so, sir," replied Esther. "No, it's just that Miss

Armstrong has decided that while we are all confined to our houses, every pupil may dress as we do after Chapel on a Sunday, when we can wear mufti. Her edict came out just after we got the two classes across to the classrooms, which is why you saw the girls there in uniform."

"I see. Right, gentlemen. Inspector, when you've finished talking to the people in Wollstonecraft, please ask someone to show you to Pankhurst. Gemmill, you move on to Nightingale. I'll take Fry. When you get back from the buses, Borthwick, you can take Austen – that'll probably have to be after dinner this evening.

"All clear? Good. Lead on please, ladies."

As they moved off, it was noticeable that Alice, the DCI's escort, was nearly as tall as him, whereas Pamela was a good foot shorter than Inspector Davison. The two other girls were of similar height to the sergeants, but considerably less wide.

Adair wondered whether he should have cautioned the two younger men about not flirting or otherwise getting familiar with the indisputably pretty girls, but decided that he could trust them both to behave professionally.

Alice chattered away as they walked along.

"We all hope Megan and Aaliyah are found very soon," she said, "even though that'll mean we have to get back to school. It's very worrying – although I think the youngest girls haven't really understood the possible dangers."

"No," agreed Adair, "but perhaps that's just as well.

"Tell me about your Housemistress – Lovelace isn't one of the houses with a married couple in charge, I believe?"

That's right, sir. We have Miss Fleming as Housemistress, and Miss Bennett as House Tutor. They're all right, and they give my fellow-prefects Leah and Francesca and me backing when necessary. Miss Fleming teaches music, and is in charge of the choir. She's a real whizz on the piano, and on the chapel organ. Miss Bennett is mainly science, but takes maths classes occasionally if another teacher is sick. She's really good at explaining things.

"We're also very lucky in Lovelace in that our cook Mrs Burton is reckoned to be the best of the eight. You'll see in a few minutes."

"Presumably you know Aaliyah pretty well?"

"Only up to a point. You can't help getting to know everyone to a certain level when you're shut in with them day after day for two thirds of the year. And she's been in my house for over three years. I usually preside over her table for meals. But apart from that, I don't actually speak to her that often. When she was younger and lived in the junior common room, I already had a study, and by the time I became a prefect and had to supervise the girls in the common room she had been allotted a study of her own.

"Anyway, here we are, sir."

Adair saw that Lovelace House was a large brick building, erected he guessed in about 1905. He noted that there were three very similar houses not far away.

Alice saw where he was looking, and explained a little more.

"You can't see the other four houses from here – they're just behind that wing of the main school. But to look at they are similar to these four. I think they were built a few years before ours – perhaps in the 1890s."

"I note that each bears the name of a famous woman," said the DCI.

"That's right," agreed Alice, "and they are now all named after British women. I know the names of one or two houses have been changed over the years – Burdett-Coutts used to be called Hypatia, and I believe Somerville was once Gentileschi. I really don't know who Hypatia was," she confided.

Adair smiled. All I can tell you is that she was a mathematician, astronomer, and teacher, who lived about 1500 years ago in Alexandria – which is now in Egypt but was then part of the Roman Empire. I really can't think why I've remembered that useless bit of information," he added.

"I'm a little surprised that you don't have a house named after Edith Cavell."

"Ah, yes. Miss Stott, the last Head, told us once that when the last renaming was done, the

Governors couldn't decide between Edith Cavell and Angela Burdett-Coutts, and eventually tossed a coin. It's believed though, that one of the two new houses already being planned will bear Miss Cavell's name."

As the two of them went into the house, Alice informed him that she was to show him where he was to sleep, and then take him to Miss Fleming's study. As they passed along a corridor, they met several girls, and his escort enquired if the Chief Inspector wanted to talk to any of them."

"Later, please, Alice."

She led him upstairs to a room which screamed 'sick bay', equipped with four iron bedsteads, each made up with a red blanket uppermost. He dropped his case on the floor.

"Very suitable, thank you Alice."

She led him back downstairs, and tapped on a door. There was a call of "come in".

"Chief Inspector Adair for you, miss."

"Ah, come and take a seat," said the Housemistress, rising to shake his hand. "I'm Mary Fleming. You can go, Alice. You'll be able to talk to Mr Adair later – probably over several days, as we've been lumbered with him indefinitely!"

A smile on the lady's face robbed that statement of any offence.

Adair saw another woman of similar age and appearance as the two teachers he had seen earlier. Another indirect casualty of the war, he guessed. A striking feature, which he had immediately noted on shaking hands, was Miss Fleming's unusually long fingers. He had no idea whether this characteristic made playing a keyboard instrument easier, but told himself that he would have guessed the lady's skill even if Alice hadn't mentioned it.

"We have a few minutes before lunch, Chief Inspector. Do you want to interrogate me now, or shall we just have a chat?"

"A chat would be fine, ma'am. Thank you for accommodating me; the room is ideal. And Alice tells me that your cook is the best in the school."

"So it's said. But as I never get to eat in the other houses, I can't confirm the rumour. As far as the hospitality is concerned, we housemistresses received our orders. That said, I'd have jumped at the chance of having a Scotland Yard officer visiting my house!

"My House Tutor, Jacqueline Bennett, and I are at your disposal, of course. As we aren't in school – we're effectively locked down as if the Black Death is stalking the countryside – we're free at almost any time.

"You'll want to speak to the girls, of course. If you want to see them individually, we can arrange that. And of course you can speak to those nearest to you over meals. At lunch now, you've been placed on the top table, with me and the oldest girls. But for dinner tonight I thought you might like to sit with those nearer to Aaliyah's age."

"Most considerate; thank you."

"Tell me, Chief Inspector, if it isn't confidential, what you think has happened to our two missing girls."

"I'm sorry to say that I fear they have been abducted, ma'am. The school premises have been thoroughly searched and there is no sign of them. I understand – and you may be able to confirm this – that the two were not in the habit of going around together. So it seems very unlikely that they have absconded. How this abduction was done is not yet evident. Nor why – and although it may seem an odd thing to say, one can only hope it is a matter of issuing a demand for a ransom, and not any other reason."

"Amen to that. You presumably think that this is an 'inside job', so to speak?"

"Hard to see how it could be otherwise. While an outsider – say a delivery man with a van – might conceivably snatch one girl. It's almost beyond belief to think that he could grab and overpower one, and then go back for a second.

"And then there's the point that these two are from among the richest families in the land. That could be coincidence, but it probably isn't.

"I rather think that although the actual removal of the children may have been done by an outsider, there was very probably inside help."

Miss Fleming nodded sadly.

"Did you speak to Aaliyah yesterday, perhaps at breakfast or lunch, or during the morning break?" enquired Adair.

"Not at either meal, certainly, and I don't remember doing so at any other time here in the house. As for at school, no again. I had no lessons yesterday morning, and didn't go into school until the afternoon.

"We need to go to lunch, Chief Inspector."

Adair was led into a very pleasant dining room, which had five tables, at each of which were seven or eight girls standing behind their chairs. A lady – the DCI assumed it was Miss Bennett, presided over what was evidently the most junior table, and a prefect was at the head of each of the other three – Alice heading what might be called Table 4. Miss Fleming indicated that the DCI should go to the foot of her table, and then glanced across to see that the other tables were all ready before saying Grace.

"Benedictus, Benedicat."

There was a noisy shuffling of chairs as everyone sat down, but the Housemistress remained standing.

"The gentleman on my table is Detective Chief Inspector Adair, from Scotland Yard in London. You all know why he and his men are here. A few of you have already met him, and he'll speak to many of you later today or tomorrow. Carry on."

There was an immediate buzz of conversation from each table.

Adair smiled at the girls on his table, all of

whom looked to be sixteen or seventeen, and who were staring at him curiously.

"You know who I am," he said to the ones to his immediate left and right. "How about telling me your names, and the names of your colleagues?"

"I'm Sarah Hodge," said the girl to his left, and going along on my side of the table we have Becky Rawlinson, Annette Winfarthing, and Deirdre Simpson."

"And I'm Fenella Williams, and the others on my side are Polly Rushton, Amanda Wynn-Jones, and Evelyn Jennings."

Miss Fleming was loading pieces of meat onto plates, which were then being passed down the table. Fenella put the first plate down in front of the DCI.

"Help yourself to vegetables and gravy, sir," she instructed him.

"You'll never remember all those names, will you sir?" enquired Sarah, as Adair picked up his knife and fork and was about to start on what looked like a nice piece of roast pork.

"While I'm here, I'll probably be able to retain them. Let's see – going round clockwise, you are Sarah, then Becky, Annette, Deirdre, Miss Fleming, Evelyn, Amanda, Polly, and Fenella."

"Gosh, that's impressive!" exclaimed Polly.

"Don't be too impressed, Polly. It's a memory trick, really. And twenty-four hours after leaving this job, the names will be wiped from my brain.

By that I don't want to imply that you aren't worth remembering – it's just that in my job I need to free some memory space up for some new facts."

A few moments passed while food was being chewed. Adair heard one of the girls at the far end talking to Miss Fleming.

"It's not really fair, miss – we can't talk to the Chief Inspector this far away. Can we move around after the first course?"

"A sensible suggestion, Deirdre. Yes. The easiest thing to do is for Mr Adair to come and sit in my chair, and I'll move down to his."

She caught the DCI's eye, and smiled as she called down the table.

"They don't get many chances for chatting to males, Chief Inspector. Please indulge them!"

"Are we allowed to ask you how you're getting on with finding Aaliyah and Megan?" asked Becky.

"You are certainly allowed to ask, Becky, but I can't give you much of an answer. To be frank, we don't yet know why they've disappeared, nor how they got out. As you probably know, my colleagues and I have met all the pupils who were in the last classes with the missing girls. Later, we'll be talking to anyone who might have had contact with them earlier – between breakfast and lunch. And of course we're speaking to all the staff too."

"But you must suspect that they've been kidnapped, don't you, sir?" asked Sarah. "After all, Miss Armstrong must think that, or she wouldn't be keeping us locked up in the houses."

"Yes; there's no point in denying the likelihood of that possibility – but it's equally pointless for any of you to dwell on it."

Adair stopped speaking while he took a few more bites of his lunch.

"Now, I appreciate you are all older, but did any of you know Aaliyah particularly well? We're trying to find out what might have been in her mind yesterday."

All the girls within earshot shook their heads.

"Even a one-year age difference is significant in the house – and in the school, for that matter," said Fenella. "Three years is a chasm. We don't eat together, we don't have lessons together, we don't play games together, we don't share studies. In assembly, or in chapel, we don't sit together."

"That's right," called Annette from further up the table. "We speak to younger ones occasionally, of course, but one doesn't get to be close friends. I think the two who might be closest to Aaliyah are Phoebe and Geraldine – they're on the second table over there." She waved vaguely over her shoulder.

"Thank you, Annette. Yes, I've spoken to both of them. But you are absolutely right to mention it – don't any of you omit to tell me anything because you think I've probably heard it already!"

Everyone had now finished their main

course, and the plates were being passed along both sides of the table to Deirdre and Evelyn, who stacked them. A maid then came to clear them away, while another brought a large metal dish which appeared to contain some sort of sponge pudding. Miss Fleming ordered that it and the pile of dessert plates should be placed in front of "the gentleman at the far end", and she then rose to change places with the DCI.

The conversation with the girls now nearer to him added nothing to his investigation. He really enjoyed the baked sponge jam pudding, and noted aloud that the custard was not lumpy in the way he recalled school custard had been in his day.

Miss Fleming heard this remark, and called down the table.

"I abhor lumpy custard," she said. "There's no excuse for it. Cook knows my views," she added meaningfully, and all the girls on the table smiled.

CHAPTER 6

The Housemistress had been keeping an eye on the rest of the dining room. Now, having decided that everyone had finished eating, she stood up, everyone immediately following suit and pushing their chairs under the table. When all was silent again, Miss Fleming spoke:

After Grace, all the third-year girls are to remain here in the dining room. The Chief Inspector will want to talk to you as a group, and he may want to see some of you individually later.

She bowed her head.

"Benedicto, benedicatur."

The girls started to file out of the room in a fairly orderly manner, the older ones leading. Six girls remained.

Miss Fleming came up to the DCI with the other teacher in tow.

"This is Jacqueline Bennett, our House Tutor." The two shook hands. Adair saw a slim woman wearing a pleasant smile. He guessed that she was still just on the right side of thirty, and thought that this young spinster would not have been affected by the war in the same way that some of the others had.

"When you've finished in here, Chief Inspector, ask one of the girls to show you to Jackie's room – she'll be waiting to be interrogated. Then, if you need anything more from me, I'll be around somewhere. I'll see you at half past six for dinner, if not before."

The two teachers left the room, and Adair turned back to the six pupils, still standing beside their table.

"Please sit down – gather at this end," he told them, as he took the chair at the head. "Now, I've spoken to Geraldine and Phoebe before, but I don't know the rest of you." He turned to his left, where a diminutive freckled girl with red hair and green eyes was looking at him. "Would you introduce yourself and your colleagues, please?"

"I'm Mary O'Donnell, sir. To my left is Anne Hazel, and next to her is Geraldine, as you know. Opposite Gerry is Olive Seymour, then Phoebe, and on your right is Athene Fitzwallace."

"Forgive my asking, Mary, but in Aaliyah's class I saw a girl who looked a lot like you – but I don't think it was you. Was it?"

"Not me, sir; my sister Ciara. We're twins – not identical but very alike. The school policy is to put siblings in different houses, and although we're in the same class for some subjects, we aren't together for History."

"I see, thank you. Now, you all know what

has happened. Or rather what we think has happened. Gerry here says that Aaliyah seemed to be more excited after the mid-morning break. I'm interested in what she might have said to anyone that day. Did anyone see her talking to an adult – not necessarily a teacher – at any time that morning – but particularly during that break?"

All six girls shook their heads.

"All right. It seems Aaliyah visited the lavatory during that break. Did any of you go at the same time?"

Again the heads shook.

"I don't know about anyone else," remarked Athene, a girl who looked to be twice the size of Mary, "but I go soon after breakfast and usually not again until lunchtime."

This time the remaining five heads nodded in agreement.

"I'm sorry to harp on about this," said Adair, "but do teachers and pupils share the same toilet facilities in the school?"

"They have their own near the staff room, sir," replied Anne, "but they quite often use ours in the classroom blocks because it's quite a way back to theirs. Not Mr Redpath, of course."

"That's helpful, thank you."

There was a silence for a minute, and then Geraldine spoke.

"It's pretty clear what you suspect, sir. Aaliyah might have been promised something after school – and if so it must have been by someone she really trusted. Couldn't have been someone like – I don't know – the baker. I can't even see her going with someone like Green, either."

"You're right that we are treating that as a possibility, Gerry. But we can't say that's what definitely happened."

"If she met someone in the lavatory, that pretty well rules out tradesmen like the baker – and Green too for that matter," said Olive. A man in the female toilets would be rather noticeable!"

"Good point," agreed the DCI. "Do any of you have any other ideas – alternative theories, if you like – about what might have happened?"

After a few moments of silence, Mary spoke again.

"Could they have just walked down the drive to the road, and caught a bus?"

"A good thought, Mary. We are indeed checking with the bus company to see if any girls boarded a bus by the school gates yesterday. However, it doesn't seem at all likely. If it had only been one girl, she might have absconded. But two – who don't seem to be particularly close friends – doing that together? And where would they go? But we have to check every possibility.

"Now, I have a question which I should have asked Miss Armstrong. But you girls may have a better idea of the answer than she does.

"Which adults in the school have motor cars or to your knowledge can drive? Not just the teachers. Consult among yourselves."

There was immediate chattering across the table. After a minute, Mary, who although the smallest seemed to be something of a leader, was deputed to speak.

"Among the resident staff, Mrs and Mr Harvey in Pankhurst House have a car, and both of them can drive. Dr Livermore has a car, but we don't think Mrs Livermore can drive. Mr Redpath in Austen has a car, but his wife definitely can't drive. Painter, the groundsman, drives the little tractor around pulling the mower or a cart, so he knows how to drive but he doesn't have a car. Green, the junior groundsman, has a motorcycle. We don't know if any of the other staff can drive, but as far as we know nobody else has a car.

"We're not a hundred percent sure about the staff who don't live here, but we know Miss Townsend has a car. We think Mr Dodds is the only other one with a car. He drives an old Riley Redwing, and comes to work in it every day. Lovely car, really – all silver and red. I'd love to go for a ride in it – in the summer with the top down, anyway. We know two or three teachers come by bicycle, and others who travel by bus."

"Useful; thanks. Does the school have any transport – a bus or anything?"

"No, sir," replied Mary. "At the beginning and end of term Aldis puts on one of his buses between the railway station and the school, making as many journeys as necessary. If some of us are being taken somewhere – say to a museum – again a bus is hired from Aldis."

"I had to be taken to hospital once," interjected Anne. "It wasn't bad enough to call for an ambulance, so they called a taxicab. That was under the previous Head, but I've seen Miss Armstrong call a taxi for herself."

Adair nodded slowly. "Thank you girls; that's all useful information. I need hardly say that if anything else comes to mind, however trivial it may seem to be, please come and find me. You can all carry on now."

The six girls pushed back their chairs and rose, all giving the DCI a smile as they left the table. Mary – inevitably – waited to show him to the House Tutor's room.

The diminutive girl led him along a corridor, and tapped on a door. Opening it on the call of "come in" she announced "Chief Inspector Adair, miss," before scurrying away.

The room was much the same size as that of the Housemistress, and similarly furnished. A large desk was placed so the user could look straight out of the window, where there was an unobstructed view of the grounds. Two comfortable armchairs were placed either side of the fireplace. The House Tutor rose to greet the DCI.

"Welcome to my little retreat, Chief Inspector. Do take a seat. I can make you a cup of tea if you fancy one?"

"Thank you, no. Just a five-minute chat, if

you please."

"Okay. This is a fine kettle of fish," she added, sitting down in the second armchair and looking at Adair expectantly.

He nodded.

"It is indeed. And although we all pray that this will just turn out to be some silly prank, the reality is that the situation is very serious – potentially even fatal."

It was the teacher's turn to nod.

"I assume the searchers have found nothing?"

"No. And to be honest, I didn't expect them to. If this is a double abduction, the girls would have been miles away before their absence was even noticed."

"Yes. And no doubt some wretch will soon be issuing a demand for money."

"It seems likely," agreed Adair. "However, we're working on the theory that someone promised these two girls some sort of treat, and that this offer was made on the morning they disappeared. Since you – and most of the other teachers – were in a staff meeting and so have alibis, I'm not accusing you of being involved. But perhaps, without even realising the significance of it, you saw someone talking to Aaliyah or Megan yesterday morning?"

"I wish I had, and could tell you. Being her House Tutor I know Aaliyah very well, of course, but I don't teach her in school this year. I know

Megan because I taught her last year and the year before, but again she isn't in any of my classes this year. To be honest, I don't remember seeing either of those two in school at any time yesterday. Aaliyah was here for breakfast and lunch, but she doesn't sit at my table, and I didn't speak to her yesterday."

She thought for a minute, staring unseeingly at the fireplace, which was laid ready for the fire to be lit.

"You've spoken to Gerry Wyatt and Phoebe Brent-Williams, I think," she said at last. "They were her closest friends. If they don't know anything, I doubt if anybody does. But what sort of treat could anyone offer? And who, apart from a teacher, would they trust? These two are very far from being stupid children, and all the girls are taught to be wary of strangers."

There was a knock on the door, and a girl, evidently one of the very youngest, came in. Adair didn't remember seeing her before.

"Yes, Nicole, what is it?"

"Excuse me, miss; I have a message for the Chief Inspector. There is a policeman in uniform downstairs, sir, asking to see you. He has a flat hat and silver things on his shoulder, so I think he's higher than a constable."

Adair stood up. "I'll come and see him at once, Nicole. Thank you, Miss Bennett. I'll no doubt see you again later. Lead on, young lady."

It was only a few yards back into the

big entrance hall, where Inspector Hatrick was standing beside a set of pigeon holes which the DCI guessed were for holding incoming mail. Hatrick was eyeing a large portrait of a woman whose face was looking across the stairwell.

"That's Ada, Countess of Lovelace," announced little Nicole as she saw Hatrick gazing at the portrait. "This house was named after her – they say she was very good at maths. And she was the daughter of Lord Byron, who was a famous poet, and friends with Mary Somerville who also has a house named after her."

Adair smiled at this brief biography.

"Thank you, Nicole, you run along now. What have you to report, Inspector?"

"No trace of either girl, sir. I just came to say that Colonel Hardy has agreed to call off the search. I've stood the civilian helpers down. However, the Chief wants a number of both CID and uniformed officers to start going round Davyton and the nearby villages tomorrow, just asking if people saw the girls – perhaps in a car – yesterday.

"Oh, and the Chief said he'll come and talk to you later today. Any progress here, sir?"

"Not really. We believe someone promised them a treat, and as a result they walked out of the building and presumably went off with someone. But as yet we have no idea who."

"I suppose there'll be a ransom demand in a day or two. I just hope the children aren't harmed. Anyway, I'll be off. Anything you need, sir, just call me."

"Thanks, Inspector, I will. You've been looking at the plans of the school – can you remember which is Fry House?

"Yes; it's the next one along – fifty yards away over there," he said pointing.

"I'll show you, sir, and introduce you to Miss Jekyll if she's in," said a female voice. Adair realised that Alice Prendergast had materialised behind him.

"Very kind. I may see you later, Inspector. Lead on, Alice."

"May I ask how you're getting on, sir," asked the prefect.

"Not much progress since I last spoke to you," admitted the DCI with a grim smile. We're looking for anyone who saw Aaliyah talking to an adult – any sort of adult – yesterday morning between breakfast and lunch. No luck with that as yet."

"I see; well, I'll ask around. I sat with her contemporaries at breakfast and lunch today, and listened to their conversations. It was pretty obvious they were all mystified. Here we are, sir," she added, pulling open the front door of a house which was clearly contemporaneous with Lovelace, and externally at least appeared identical.

Internally too, it seemed, because the Housemistress's room here was in exactly the same position as Miss Fleming's. Alice tapped on the door, and put her head inside the room.

"I've brought Chief Inspector Adair, Miss."

"Ah, we've been expecting a visit from someone; thank you, Alice. Do come in, Chief Inspector.

Entering the room, the DCI saw there were actually two women present, both very similar in both age – late-forties – and appearance. His immediate thought was that these were more indirect casualties of the war.

Welcome to Fry House; I'm Laura Jekyll, and this is Patricia Finlay, our House Tutor.

Adair spent ten minutes with the two teachers, and learned nothing new. Miss Finlay then took him to the empty dining room, where she arranged for a maid to bring him a cup of tea, while she went off to find those girls in the house who were in the same year as Megan and Aaliyah. Two girls arrived at the same time as the tea, and had only just introduced themselves and sat down when three more came in in quick succession.

"That's the lot, sir," said the last one, "there are only five of us third-years in this house."

The DCI spent fifteen minutes with this group, and although the girls were almost pathetically eager to help, they had no additional information. Eventually, Adair sent them away with thanks, and sat in contemplation for a few minutes. Then he got up and carried his empty cup through to the kitchen, where he found a surprisingly youthful Cook sitting at a table in a side room, with some papers in front of her. Introducing himself, and apologising for disturbing her, he asked the same question that he had put to the Cook in Lovelace House earlier.

"Bless you, sir, I'm glad to be distracted. We have a couple of hours free before it's time to start preparing dinner, and I thought I'd just do a bit of paperwork. Mr Dodds does most of the ordering of food and so on, but we cooks obviously have to tell him what's needed.

"In answer to your question, yes, there were four tradesmen here yesterday – milkman, butcher, baker, and the general grocer. Some days we have the fishmonger and the greengrocer, but not yesterday. Each of the men yesterday would have called at all eight houses. But they all came in the morning, well before lunch. I can't guarantee it, but I don't think that any of them would have come back in the afternoon. Nor would any other tradesman. I hear these girls disappeared after four o'clock, and it was getting dark by then. I've never known anyone to deliver in the dark. It's always in the morning."

After a few more minutes of conversation, Adair thanked the Cook, found his way out of the building without meeting anyone, and walked back to the old house.

He found the Secretary in her office, looking in the drawer of a filing cabinet.

"Sorry, Chief Inspector, I had to come in to find a file. I won't be a minute."

Don't worry, Miss Spencer, my colleagues aren't back yet so you aren't disturbing our work. But while you're here, I'd like to pick your brains. Come and sit down when you have your file – this won't take long."

Miss Spencer ruffled through items in the drawer, and quickly brought out a folder. She dropped it on her desk, and then took a seat on the opposite side to the one she normally occupied. Smiling, Adair sat in her usual chair.

"I'm interested in people with cars," he explained. "Not just teachers – anybody here. Some of the children have given me a list, but they admitted it might not be complete. So I'd like you to do the same. As best you can."

The Secretary nodded understandingly. She reached across the desk for a pad, and started to write. Within a minute she tore off a sheet, and pushed it across to the DCI.

"There are very few car-owners here, Chief Inspector. I don't think I've missed anyone."

Adair glanced at the list, written in a very neat hand. "Thank you for this, Miss Spencer. I'm pleased to say that it is exactly the same as one provided by the girls in Lovelace House."

"But surely Aaliyah and Megan couldn't have been taken away in one of these cars? You can't think that a teacher or indeed any of our people is responsible for this outrage?"

"At the moment, I don't think anything. But you'll appreciate that I must consider every possibility, however unlikely. After all, the disappearance of two girls was pretty unlikely."

"What about tradesmen and people in their vans?"

"Oh yes, we're looking at them. But it seems that yesterday they all came in the morning – and both girls were certainly still here at four o'clock."

"Oh dear; yes, I see. Will you excuse me now, Chief inspector – the Head wants this file."

"Of course, Miss Spencer, thank you. Just one more thing – would you know where Mr Dalby is at present? He isn't a suspect, but I want to see everyone eventually, and I might as well start on that until my men get back."

"He could be almost anywhere in the school, or in one of the houses. But he has a workshop in a sort of shed attached to the swimming pool. You could try there. Or hold on for a moment, and I'll ask Mr Dodds. He's in charge of Dalby, and might know what he's doing at present."

The Secretary left the room via the other interconnecting door, and was back within a minute.

"Bill doesn't know – he also suggests you try the workshop. Can you find it?"

Adair said that the swimming pool had already been pointed out to him, and started on his way. However, on going around the first corner in the corridor, he almost collided with a short man in a dark overcoat hurrying in the opposite direction. Both started to apologise, and then stopped.

"Are you DCI Adair?" asked the wiry man.

"I am – and I guess you must be Colonel Hardy?"

"Quite right." The Chief Constable put out his hand.

"Where can we talk? I'll not keep you long."

"Miss Armstrong has lent us her Secretary's office, sir – follow me."

Hardy took off his overcoat, and the DCI saw he wasn't in uniform, but was wearing a charcoal grey suit. The two men sat down and each quickly appraised the other. The DCI saw a man in his fifties with greying hair cut *en brosse*, possessing a very determined-looking face on which a neat moustache seemed to fit perfectly.

"Any progress?" enquired the Chief Constable. "You'll have heard that the search has produced nothing."

"Very little as yet, sir," replied Adair. "We know that both girls attended their last class as expected. We know that one was walking towards a back door a few minutes later. We are also told that one was showing signs of excitement – she mentioned a 'treat' but unfortunately didn't expand on that. We've been talking to the children and staff, of course, and that exercise is ongoing. We're checking with the bus company, in case the girls boarded a bus by the school gates."

Hardy grunted. "If your supposition is right, and these children were bribed in some way, then

I suppose they'd have been sworn to secrecy." He shook his head sadly.

"Look, I don't want to hold you up, and I don't expect a written report every day. Just keep me informed of any progress – or if there's a development such as a ransom demand. Obviously, you must ask if you need any assistance – Hatrick will help if you ask. I've got him carrying out a wider search tomorrow, although I accept it's probably useless."

The telephone rang just as Hardy stopped speaking. With an apology, the DCI picked up the receiver, assuming that the call would turn out to be for the Secretary.

"Willowbank School, may I help you? Yes… Oh, yes, Inspector…I see…Well, thank you for that…I'll talk to him myself…Goodbye."

Replacing the receiver, Adair looked at the Chief Constable.

"Inspector Hatrick, sir. One of his constables involved in the search of the grounds earlier today just happened to walk past one of the groundsmen working on something. They didn't speak to the man. Your officer thought he'd seen him before, but it took a few hours before he remembered where.

"It seems the man, whose name is Green, was convicted of larceny at Quarter Sessions a little over two years ago. He got a twelve-month sentence."

"Hopeful, you think?"

"Not greatly, sir, no. He lives in one of the lodges by the gate, and that has already been searched. Also, assuming abduction, it would seem that a motor vehicle must have been used. Green has a motor cycle, but no car or van. I'll interview him, of course."

Hardy grunted again. "All right, carry on. I'll go and talk to the Head. A good woman, that."

CHAPTER 7

Adair was about to restart his visit to find Dalby, when Davison and Gemmill returned together. He sat down again, and motioned his colleagues to do the same.

"How have you been getting on – both had a decent lunch, I hope?"

"Not bad, sir," replied the Inspector, "but the children in the second house I visited told me that the best cook is in Lovelace – where you went, I think. But as they all said they'd never eaten there, I'm not sure how the ranking is done!"

"Well, I've eaten better and worse, sir," said Gemmill. "But I'm not dreading future meals, anyway."

"All right. Anything of vital importance to report?"

"Perhaps, sir," said Davison. "Going back about fourteen years, before I joined the Met, I was a uniformed constable in Essex. I had to give evidence at the Assizes in Chelmsford. My case was due to start after lunch, as the judge had to finish off some earlier cases in the morning. I was very green – had never even given evidence before the magistrates. So my inspector told me to go and sit in court and watch, 'to pick up the atmosphere', as he put it.

"The judge had two sentencing matters to deal with. One was a chap who'd pleaded guilty to a charge of bigamy. He got forty-two months, and the judge said it would have been a good bit more if he hadn't pleaded guilty, and if he had had previous convictions of any sort.

"The man's name was Reynolds, and I can still picture him very clearly. A very good-looking young man – 'distinguished' is probably the right word. Today, I saw Mr & Mrs Harvey, in Pankhurst House. I gathered that Mrs Harvey – April – is the Housemistress, and her husband just helps.

"But I'm pretty good at faces, sir, and I'm almost certain that Jonathan Harvey was the man I saw sent down under the name of Reynolds all those years ago."

"Did he see that you recognised him?

"No, sir. After the first few seconds when I clocked him, I hardly looked at him. And he only spoke a few words – his wife did all the talking."

"Hmm," muttered the DCI. "I've been asking about who has a car. The Harveys do – and although Mrs Harvey was attending a staff meeting after school, her husband – who only married her quite recently – isn't a teacher and so is unaccounted for. We'll need to talk to him. Well remembered, Inspector.

"A similar bit of memory by one of the local men suggests that the assistant groundsman, Green, has a conviction for larceny, and served twelve months. Somehow one doesn't expect a place like this to have ex-cons around. But I wonder whether the Head knows about Green – and I also wonder whether Mrs Harvey knows about her husband's previous – if he is Reynolds.

"Anything else emerge?"

Both men shook their heads.

"All right. I think we'll change the arrangements again. Borthwick isn't back yet, so Gemmill, you find out where Austen House is, and go and talk to people there. I'm leaving all the cooks and maids for the moment, largely on the basis that they are all women, and I can't see this as being female-led. But we do need to talk to Messrs Dalby, Painter, and of course Green. We'll leave Harvey for the moment until we can check him out.

"You carry on with Austen, Sergeant. After we've all eaten in our respective houses, I suggest we meet here again. I guess that'll be about seven-thirty. Off you go now.

"Right, Inspector. Do you have any useful contacts in Essex?"

"Yes sir, my oldest friend is a DI based in Chelmsford."

"Good. Get on the phone, and see if you can find him. Ask if he can help with digging out the old records on Reynolds. A photograph would be good; prints would be even better. Also, it would be interesting to know if the proper wife is still alive, or if they divorced or something. Not really a job for your friend, that – we may have to do other searches. But get her name from the file, if possible."

"Okay, sir. But she'd only be about forty now, so probably still alive. Also, when Reynolds' counsel was mitigating, I remember he said that the reason his client committed bigamy was that although they were separated, the real wife wouldn't agree to divorce – apparently on religious grounds. If that remained the situation, he may well have another bigamous marriage now."

Davison picked up the telephone. As he began to explain to the operator what he wanted, Borthwick entered the room.

"While Mr Davison is on the telephone, tell me quietly how you got on," instructed Adair.

"I spoke to Mr and Mrs Redpath in Burdett-Coutts House, sir, and also the Tutor, Miss Roisin McCullough. Can't say I warmed to the Redpaths – a bit stand-offish they are – but the Irish girl is a red-haired beauty of about thirty, and really pleasant.

"Mrs R had a hospital appointment at twenty to five. She doesn't drive, so her husband took her in his car. They left at about ten past four, and went out via the front gates. Apparently it takes about twenty minutes to drive from the school to the hospital, so as they said there wasn't much time to spare between the end of the last lesson and the appointment. Time being short, Redpath had parked his car by the front door of the school, all ready to dash off as soon as their respective lessons were finished. He says that when they left the only other car by the front door was the Bursar's.

"I had a decent lunch in the House, and was entertained by some nice kids. After lunch I spoke to all the girls in the house who are in the same year as Megan and Aaliyah. Nobody knew anything, and I didn't see any sign that anyone was concealing information.

"Then I thought that I'd try to contact the bus company by telephone, so I came in here and got hold of a supervisor at the garage. The whole thing was very easy. As you thought, sir, the only suitable buses in either direction pass the gates here within ten minutes of each other – one at four fifteen, and the other going the other way at four twenty-four. And the same crews were working today as were on yesterday. So I parked by the gates, and waited. I stopped each bus in turn, and spoke to its driver and conductor. All four men said that no child got on the bus that day – neither bus was required to stop at all yesterday. In fact none of them could remember the last time a child boarded one of those two buses.

"But before I went to the bus stops, sir, I took the car and found the hospital. I made enquiries, and there is no doubt whatsoever that Mr and Mrs

Redpath were in the car when it arrived at the hospital somewhere around half-past four. There is a man sitting in a kiosk at the hospital car park. His job is to make sure that only senior staff – consultants, registrars, and the matron – get into the tiny car park. He remembered the Redpaths, because after a minute of argument he let Redpath park – there were several spare spaces at that time of the afternoon, and Mrs R said her appointment was urgent. The man had a note of the car and number, and I've subsequently checked – it was Redpath's car.

"The attendant is adamant that there were no children in the car. I suppose the missing girls could have been locked in the boot, sir, but that doesn't seem likely."

"No, it doesn't. But I suppose the two could have been dropped off somewhere on the way – but if so the Redpaths would have surely said something by now.

"All right, Sergeant, you've done very well."

Davison had put down the telephone, and briefly explained about his conversation.

"My friend is very happy to see what he can dig up. He's in the same building as where the records are stored, but he has no idea how long it'll take to find what we want. Perhaps an hour, perhaps a week. He'll call back anyway.

"He suggested that if the details of the first wife are in the file, there might be a chance that she still lives at the same address. If so, he'll get someone to call on her."

"Excellent, Inspector. Right, change of plans. You don't need to go to Austen after all, Sergeant – Gemmill has gone to do that. I want you to go and find Bailey, the chap who lives on the top floor here. Then find the other odd-job man, Dalby, and talk to him. He may be in his workshop, which is attached to the swimming pool building. After that, go back to your house. We're meeting here after the evening meal, say about half past seven.

"Inspector, see if you can find Painter, the head groundsman. Probably in his lodge by now, by the main gate. Take a car – I don't want you falling over in the dark and breaking something!

"I'm going to pay a courtesy visit on the Head. Incidentally, the Chief Constable was here a few minutes ago. If you see a short man in mufti, with a moustache, that's probably him. Don't salute, of course, but come to attention and call him 'sir'. Okay, carry on."

Adair tapped on the interconnection door to the Headmistress's room. There was a muffled call of "come in", and he went through to find, as expected, Miss Armstrong at her desk with Colonel Hardy sitting facing her.

Hardy rose as the DCI came in. "I'll go, Lucy, and leave you to be interrogated. Call me tomorrow when convenient, Adair."

"Actually, Rupert, I wonder if you'd stay at least for a minute or two. I'd like to take soundings from both of you. Is that in order, Chief Inspector?"

"Certainly, ma'am. I'm only making a courtesy call anyway."

"Do take a seat, then. No news, I assume?"

"Not really, ma'am. But there are a couple of things which have emerged during our enquiries. Pardon me, Colonel, but have you briefed the Head on anything? I don't want to tell her the same thing twice."

"Certainly not, Adair, I know I'm in an odd position here, but I don't pass on police business to anyone."

"Apologies, sir. Well, ma'am, we have learned that Megan became quite excited at some point during yesterday morning. She mentioned to a friend something about looking forward to a 'treat'. That is all we have, but it does seem likely to be significant. She was also last seen heading for a back door which doesn't lead in the direction of her house.

"I've personally seen all the other girls in the last classes attended by the missing pair. Between the three of us we have also spoken to most of the few others in the same year who weren't in those classes, and one of my sergeants is currently in Austen House finishing that task.

"We have checked that the girls didn't board a bus by the school gates.

"You mentioned that three teachers missed the staff meeting. Mr and Mrs Redpath did indeed attend the hospital, and so appear to be in the clear. I'll see Miss Townsend tomorrow.

"Now, your man Green, ma'am. What do you know about him?"

"Very little, really. As I said before, he was taken on by my predecessor. I have had very little contact with him, to be honest. The teachers who handle games and so on would know him better, but even they probably deal with Painter, and then I suppose Painter gives Green his instructions. Certainly from what I've seen of him he seems a very quiet young man. I've not heard of any complaint against him – not of any sort. Why do you ask?"

"It is believed that he has a criminal conviction, ma'am, for some sort of larceny, and that he has served a term of imprisonment. There is no reason to think he has any involvement with the current matter, though."

Miss Armstrong stared at the DCI. "News to me," she declared. "And if Frances Stott, my predecessor, was aware of it, I think she would have told me. What do you want me to do?"

"Nothing – for now anyway. I can't see how he could be involved in this. His house has been searched, and he'd have had a job abducting two girls on his motorcycle. It's up to you, of course, but if the young man's work is satisfactory, I think it would be rather unfair to dismiss him now."

"Yes, I suppose so. I'll inform the Chairman of Governors, but nobody else need know. Is there anything else?"

"Well, there is something else – an even

more delicate matter. However, I'm not yet sure of the facts, and until we've checked them out I can't discuss it. But as in the case of Green, I doubt if it has anything to do with the missing children."

"Sounds intriguing, Chief Inspector. Now, perhaps I can ask your advice. I emphasise that I just want your opinions – at the end of the day what I decide to do will be entirely my decision. But I'd welcome your views. You, Rupert, have two hats, but it is as a grandparent of one of our pupils that I speak to you. You Chief Inspector, are unencumbered with concern for a specific child, but you may have a view as a responsible member of the public as well as being a senior police officer.

"I can't keep the girls effectively locked in their houses much longer, and I'm contemplating returning to normal working tomorrow. Views, gentlemen?"

Hardy indicated that the DCI should speak first.

"No guarantees, ma'am, but I'll be astounded if any other girls disappear. The risk involved in taking Aaliyah and Megan must have been considerable. With police around the school, and on the gates, and all the girls on the *qui vive*, I judge it practically impossible for anyone to snatch another child. Also, it must be difficult to keep even two girls prisoner – the problems of taking in more must surely be insurmountable."

"I concur, Lucy," said Hardy. "But I have to point out you will be taking on a great responsibility if you go ahead – our support will count for nothing."

"Of course. Well, I'll think about this in the next hour or two, and make my decision. Thank you, gentlemen."

The two police officers left the Head's study, and parted after a brief word in the corridor. Adair returned to the Secretary's office, and sat down to think. Ten minutes later, no flash of inspiration had come to him, but he came out of his reverie as the telephone bell jangled. He picked up the receiver automatically, although even as he did so realised that the call would certainly be for the Secretary if not for the Headmistress. However, he was wrong. After the DCI starting off by giving the school's name, the caller then asked to speak to Inspector Davison. Adair then identified himself, and discovered that he was talking to Detective Inspector Goddard in Chelmsford, returning Davison's earlier call.

"I found the file on Reynolds easily enough sir. There are indeed prints, and a photograph. Barry asked if there were any details on the original wife – well there is a name and address. A good few years ago now, but she lives or lived here in Chelmsford, so I've got a man going around to the address now to see."

"That's extraordinarily good of you," said Adair. "Many thanks. I'll send someone up from the Yard to borrow your prints and the mugshot, if that's all right. Probably this evening, if you could leave the stuff at your front desk."

"No problem, sir. And I'll let you know if the wife is still legally married to Reynolds."

Adair cleared the line, and then immediately asked the operator to connect him with Scotland Yard. After hearing a few clicks and buzzing sounds, he was able to speak to a detective sergeant.

"Adair here, Foster. Get a DC or someone to go to Essex police headquarters immediately. He should ask for DI Goddard. If Goddard has gone home, he'll have left an envelope at the front desk. I want that envelope brought to me at Willowbank School in Kent this evening. Got that?"

DS Foster confirmed that he had 'got that', and the call was ended. The DCI went back to his thoughts. No flashes of inspiration had come to him when, some twenty minutes later, his three colleagues returned in quick succession. None had anything meaningful to report.

Adair updated them on the matter of Reynolds/Harvey, emphasising that not only was it not yet certain that the identification was correct, but that even if that were proved it still didn't necessarily have anything to do with the abductions.

"It'll soon be time to go back to our respective houses to eat, gentlemen. Before we split up, let's think about tomorrow.

"Miss Armstrong is thinking about unlocking the girls in the morning, and reverting to normal school routines. If that is so, Miss Townsend will presumably be here. If the school doesn't re-open and she doesn't come in, I'll go to her home. We also have to see the Bursar, Dodds, and the ex-con Green. Provisionally, you and I will see all those together, Inspector.

"Gemmill and Borthwick, your jobs will consist of interviewing dozens of females – cooks, housemaids, kitchen maids, and so on. I'm sure that'll be a welcome change for you – not quite the same as talking to some con or tea-leaf! There is a list of names here. In the morning, divide it up between the two of you, and make a start. It won't be easy to find the maids; some work in the houses, others in this old building or the main school. You can probably interview them while they pause in their dusting, or whatever they're doing. You certainly don't need to spend more than a few minutes on each one – I'm practically certain none of them are involved – but if you see any sign of nervousness, push hard. If in doubt call Mr Davison or me.

That leaves two men. We'll see what we get from Essex regarding Harvey/Reynolds, and play that one accordingly. Assuming Doctor Livermore isn't called in to see a sick child or staff member tomorrow, I'll go and find him in his surgery.

"All clear?"

As the three officers nodded in unison, there was a tap on the door. To Adair's shout of "come in", the door opened to reveal the same prefects who had escorted the detectives before.

"If you're ready, gentlemen," said the head prefect, "we are to show you to your houses again. Each of you is invited to take a drink with your Housemistress at six o'clock. The school and house prefects in your houses are invited too. Unprecedented. But I rather doubt if we'll be offered alcohol," she added with a smile.

"Thank you, Arabella; yes, we're ready. Gentlemen, I don't feel like going out again tonight. But if any of you want a drink at the local pub after dinner, take one of the cars – but be back by half past ten at the very latest – Head's orders. Better make it ten-fifteen."

Davison looked enquiringly at the other two, who both nodded.

"Okay," he said. "Let's meet in this room at a quarter to eight.

"Sorry, miss – lead on."

CHAPTER 8

Once again, Alice chatted as she and the DCI walked back towards Lovelace House. Any progress in the case, sir?" she asked.

"Not really," replied Adair. "All detective work is slow and steady. A case sometimes takes weeks – although for the girls' sakes I pray that this one is far shorter than that."

"Are you expecting some sort of demand for their release soon?"

He looked sideways to gauge the expression on the prefect's face. Satisfied that there was no sign of pleasurable anticipation, he replied.

"Yes. In some ways that will be good; in others, bad. It could bring us more information, and it could – depending on how the demand is handled – bring about the girls' release. But it could also be a time of great danger for them."

"Yes; I understand that. If the demands go direct to Lord Trimley and Mr Hammadani, sir, do you think they'd just pay up without informing the police or the school?"

Once again Adair glanced at his companion.

"You're very sharp, Alice. I discussed that possibility with Miss Armstrong, but nobody else has mentioned it. Please don't talk about it to your colleagues.

"I haven't yet met either of the fathers. But yes, I imagine that most parents in that situation would prioritise the return of their child ahead of the desirability of catching the abductor."

"You fear that Megan and Aaliyah might be killed after the ransom is paid, because having seen their captors that'd be the safest way of never being identified?"

The two had reached the front door of Lovelace House, and the DCI stopped, and turned to face the girl.

"I'm very impressed by your grasp of reality, Alice, but please, please, don't put that idea into anybody else's head. Yes, of course it is a possibility, but it won't help if all the pupils start to worry even more than they are at present."

"I would never do that, sir. Let's go in. I expect you want to go to your room first, so I'll see you when you come down. You know where Miss Fleming's room is."

Adair trotted up the stairs to the sickbay, wondering how many other pupils had considered the outcome which Alice had outlined.

***

Ten minutes later, after a quick wash and change of shirt, he went back downstairs and knocked gently on Miss Fleming's door. To a call of "come in", he opened the door and was greeted by the Housemistress. With her was Alice, flanked by two other senior girls. He hadn't spoken to either before, but recognised them as having been presiding over two of the tables at lunch.

""Let me introduce my two house prefects, Chief Inspector – Francesca and Leah. Adair shook hands with the two girls – one a dark-haired beauty, the other fair with striking rather than classic good looks. Have you explained the hierarchy, Alice?"

"Oh yes, Miss," grinned the girl.

Miss Fleming also smiled. "Yes; I expect it's much the same here as it is in the police force. I can tell Miss Bennett what to do – although that is rarely necessary – and in theory Alice can tell these two what to do."

"Oh, she often finds that necessary, Miss," said the blonde Leah, and all four females laughed.

What can we get you to drink, Chief Inspector? I fear I only have soft drinks or sherry."

A very dry sherry if you have one, ma'am. Otherwise a lemonade or something."

Oh, I have some excellent dry sherry. On the rare occasions I entertain here, that is what I choose. Alice, please get Mr Adair a glass."

"The Head mentioned that you and your subordinates would probably visit a public house after dinner. I'm told there is a very respectable one in Davyton, only a couple of miles away."

"My three colleagues are indeed going there, ma'am, but I'm intending to have a quiet evening in – probably just lying on my bed and thinking."

"Well, the junior girls will be going to bed at half past eight, and there are some more comfortable chairs in their common room. You would be welcome to relax in there. But perhaps…"

Alice returned at that moment, and handed the DCI a glass of very pale sherry.

"Thanks, Alice."

He raised the glass. "To the early and safe return of Aaliyah and Megan."

Miss Fleming raised her own sherry glass, and the three prefects raised their glasses of what looked like lemonade.

"To their early and safe return."

There was a moment's silence, and then the Housemistress spoke again.

"I was about to ask if you play bridge, Chief Inspector?"

"I do indeed, ma'am. My wife and I belong to a bridge club. Alas, having to work quite often in the evenings and weekends, I can't get to play as much as I'd like, and Becky sometimes has to go on her own. We don't rank in the top echelon even in our modest club, although we did quite well in both the tournaments we managed to play in earlier this year. Why do you ask – are you offering a rubber?"

"Exactly that. We have a dozen or so quite keen players in this house. Jackie Bennett is one, but it's her night off and she's gone out this evening. These three reprobates all play, and we have several others – the youngest only fifteen. Now in Jackie's absence, Alice is on duty this evening, so she can't play. But Leah and Francesca here would love to have a rubber or two. Perhaps it would be good to take your mind off the case for an hour or so."

"I'd really enjoy that – thank you all very much."

The five conversed for another ten minutes, and then Miss Fleming announced that it was time to eat.

"I assumed you wouldn't really want to talk to the same girls again, so I've put you at the head of the junior table, Chief Inspector. You shouldn't have any trouble serving the meat course tonight – it's chicken, and already divided into portions. It's up to you whether you change seats again as we did at lunch. Or you could get the girls to move around.

"Let's go along to the dining room."

Adair took his place at the head of the junior table, as instructed, and smiled at the young faces looking at him curiously. He noticed that Alice was presiding over the senior table this time, and the Housemistress was at the next table down. Leah and Francesca were at the two remaining tables.

After grace, the DCI sat down, and smiled again. Eight faces, all probably eleven or twelve years old stared back.

"Before the food arrives, I'd like to know your names. I've met Nicole briefly, but that's all. At lunch, I learned the names of the senior girls, and later those in the Third Year."

He looked at the child on his left. Perhaps you'll tell me your name – just your first name – and then give me all your friends' names starting to your left."

The youngster looked nervous, but nodded. "I'm Bethany, sir."

She went around the table, naming the other seven including Nicole, and had just reached the girl to Adair's right when one maid arrived with the chicken, and another with tureens containing potatoes, carrots and cabbage.

"Miss Fleming says I'm to dish this out," said the DCI. "I should tell you that I'm not used to this – so I'll give you a job, Bethany. If as I go along you think I'm putting too much or too little on a plate, please stop me at once." The other girls giggled, and this seemed to break the ice.

When everyone had their plate, and had helped themselves to vegetables, Adair looked along the table and spoke again before starting to eat.

"Let me just see that I've got the names right." This time he started from his right, and went anti-clockwise around the table.

"Quite right, sir," called the girl at the far end on the left. "But it's a bit difficult for us to talk to you at this end – will you change seats like we saw you did at lunchtime?"

"I certainly will, Etta. Now let's do some eating, and perhaps we can talk a bit between mouthfuls."

Nine forks quickly transferred food into their owners' mouths, and there was silence at the table for a minute. Then the girl next to Bethany asked a question.

"I know you're from Scotland Yard, sir, and obviously senior. But can I ask if detectives like you have to wear uniforms sometimes?"

"A very good question, Nadine. Yes – all detectives are just ordinary policemen who happen to do their jobs in civilian clothes most of the time. It's only on rare formal or ceremonial occasions that what are called 'plain clothes' officers have to wear uniform."

He took another mouthful of food, and a few seconds later added "It's so rare, actually, that since I was promoted to chief inspector I haven't worn my uniform at all."

"Do you have pips and things on it, sir?" asked the girl to his immediate right. "My dad was in the army during the war, and he still has his uniform. It has black pips on the shoulders, but if you have those they wouldn't really show up."

"I guess your father was in the Rifle Brigade, Delphine – only rifle regiments have black badges. And you're quite right; police uniforms use silver-coloured badges, which show up very well."

Adair managed to eat some more food

before another question arrived – one which he had anticipated but hoped wouldn't be asked.

"You will get our two girls back, won't you, sir?" enquired Bethany, somewhat plaintively.

The DCI smiled at her, but tried to include all the other girls in his reply.

"Scotland Yard prides itself in being the best detective force in the world. We'll get them back for their families, for the school, and for all of you."

The conversation became more general, the girls nearer Adair seeming to have lost their initial shyness. After the first course was finished, he picked up his dessert spoon and fork, and moved to the other end of the table, to the obvious pleasure of the four girls nearer that end. Before the pudding had even been brought in, he had been asked three more questions.

After he served out the dessert – tinned apricots and what looked like whipped evaporated milk – there was a brief lull while food was (very delicately) ladled into mouths. Then another unwelcome question – one which could have come from an adult – was thrown at him.

"If Megan and Aaliyah have been taken away by some horrid person, sir, how did they know where to go? People would have seen if the man had come right into the school."

Adair hesitated before replying.

"That is exactly what my colleagues and I have been trying to find out, Dulcie. How about you girls turning yourselves into detectives, and coming up with some ideas?"

There was a buzz of conversation around the table, and the DCI took the opportunity to finish his dessert. Apricots were not his favourite fruit, and he ruefully decided that the 'cream' didn't improve their taste.

"Suppose they got a letter, or even just a note, sir, telling them to go somewhere at a certain time?" suggested Annette, now sitting on his left.

"Yes, sir – from someone they knew," called Delphine.

Adair recognised that this suggestion, unlikely though it seemed to be, would at least explain why nobody suspicious had been seen talking to either girl on the previous day.

"I saw your pigeon holes – is that what you call them? – in the hallway earlier. Is that where your letters and things are placed?"

"That's right," confirmed Annette. "But on schooldays, the postman doesn't come before we have to go across to school. So we don't get to see our letters until lunchtime – unless we happen to run back to the house to fetch a book or something during the morning break."

"It was my birthday last week, and I went back during break that day, to collect my cards and postal orders," giggled Hazel.

Adair sat still, realising that he was guilty of dereliction of duty. He should have ordered a search of the missing girls' studies – not to look for the children themselves which had already been done, but to see if there were any clues in the way of written instructions.

"That's a good suggestion, Annette, and one we're going to be looking into." Not a lie, he told himself, because the police would indeed be doing so – belatedly.

No further ideas were forthcoming, and shortly after everyone stood for grace. As Miss Fleming passed his table, he quickly whispered, with an apology, that he would be delayed for perhaps fifteen minutes.

"That's fine, Chief Inspector – we'll play three-handed until you can join us."

Next, the DCI spoke to Alice as she passed him, and asked her to wait for a moment. When everyone else had left the dining room, he asked her to show him to Aaliyah's study. The girl asked no question, and simply led him along ground-floor corridors until they reached a door. No other children were visible, but Adair could hear voices coming from other rooms in the corridor. A small card in a metal frame on this door said 'Aaliyah Hammadani'.

"Thanks, Alice," said Adair, "you carry on now."

He opened the door and found himself in a tiny room. There was just enough space for a table, two upright chairs, a small armchair, and a wall-mounted bookcase. Some papers were spread out on the table, and there were twenty or more books on the shelves – some fiction, others clearly text books. On another shelf lay an expensive looking leather writing case, and Adair took this down and opened it at the table. Apart from new paper and envelopes, and some postage stamps, there were four envelopes addressed to Aaliyah. Three were typed, one was handwritten. He drew out the letters from each in turn. All were written in English, and it was clear that the typed ones were from the girl's father, and the other from her mother. Despite the apparent formality of the typing, all four letters were warm and friendly. Each of the typed letters were hand signed, of course, and just above each signature were a few handwritten Arabic symbols – different in every letter.

Each letter was dated, and the most recent was a week old. There was nothing suspicious in any of them.

Adair eyed the book case. Sighing, he stood again and took a book down from the shelf and turning it on its edge he ruffled through it to shake out any paper that might be inside. He repeated this with the next five books. With the sixth book, which happened to be a Latin primer, he struck gold. An envelope fell out.

Quickly dropping the book, he picked up the envelope, noting it was almost identical to the three typed ones he had already seen. Pulling a small pair of tweezers from his pocket, he carefully drew out the letter, and manoeuvred it so he could read it without touching it with his fingers.

He immediately grunted with satisfaction, and eased the letter back into its envelope. He slipped that into the writing case with the other letters, and left the room with the case under his arm. Returning to his room, he locked the writing case into his own attaché case. He then went down and joined the bridge players.

Miss Fleming didn't ask any questions, but started to explain how the members of her house approached the game.

"We use natural bidding here, Chief Inspector. Not too many of the increasingly complex so-called conventions – we play for fun. Opening one of a suit on 12-13 points. A strong one no-trump opening with 16-18 points. Opening two of any suit is an indication of a very strong hand – 20 or more points. Is all that acceptable?"

"Of course, ma'am."

"Excellent. Well, we'll cut for partners."

This exercise paired Adair with the raven-haired Francesca, and Leah took her seat opposite her Housemistress.

"We are very informal in these sessions," announced Miss Fleming. Please call me Mary. May we all use your Christian name?"

"Of course, Mary, it's David."

Twenty-five minutes and two games later, the detective and his partner had taken the first rubber. True, the cards had slightly favoured them, but in the first game Francesca had surprised her partner with some unorthodox bidding, and had then gone on to play the hand perfectly. In the next game, she had again made an unusual bid, but this time the DCI was the declarer and was left to play the hand she had contracted to make. This he did efficiently, and they ended up with an overtrick.

Miss Fleming shook her head sadly, and she offered more drinks as Leah was dealing the next hand. Adair and both girls declined. Before Leah had finished the deal, there was a knock at the door, and a maid came in.

"Beg pardon, miss, but there's a policeman from London asking to see the Chief Inspector. I've brought him over here."

"Apologies – I was half expecting this," said the DCI. "I'll only be two minutes, if you'll excuse me."

He went out into the hallway with the maid, and saw one of his DCs.

"Good evening, Jackson, thanks for coming. You got the goods from Chelmsford, then?"

"Yes sir," replied the constable, handing over a large manila envelope. And Mr Goddard told me to tell you that his man had just got back from seeing the woman you know about, and she's still married to the first man. I hope you understand that, sir, 'cos I don't. Mr Goddard made me say it twice to make sure I'd tell you right."

Adair laughed. "Yes, that's understood, Jackson. Very useful information. Now, I can't offer you a bed here, I think, so you'll have to drive back to London. Stop somewhere and have some fish and chips or something. And take the car home – you don't need to take it back to the Yard tonight."

"Oh, thank you sir."

"Right, off you go. This young lady will show you back to the front door."

Without opening the envelope, Adair returned to his bridge. Apologising again for the interruption, he placed the envelope on a little table by the door, and sat down to continue playing.

The second rubber went to three games, but Francesca and Adair took it by two games to one – and the icing on the cake was a lot of extra points for a doubled small slam in the third game.

"Dear me – four games to one, and two rubbers to none," remarked Mary Fleming, sadly. "As for the points, it's a good thing we don't play for money. Even at a shilling a hundred we'd be broke!"

Leah, who didn't seem at all put out at being on the losing side, congratulated her opponents. "You perhaps had the cards in the first rubber, but we can't complain about them in the next three games. Very well done."

Adair bade the others 'goodnight', and went upstairs to his room. There, he spent a few minutes perusing the contents of the envelope from Essex. He then took five sheets of writing paper and five envelopes from Aaliyah's writing case, and spent the next ten minutes writing notes and addressing envelopes.

He went to sleep, thinking about how to deal with the mysterious letter which Aaliyah had hidden.

CHAPTER 9

In the morning, the DCI had a bath, dressed, put on another clean shirt and underclothes, and wished he had been able to bring another suit. He went downstairs, holding the five envelopes he had been addressing the night before.

Several girls -know all dressed in their formal school uniforms – were waiting near the dining room door, and among these he saw Leah and Alice, talking to each other. They greeted him with smiles, and Alice spoke as soon as morning greetings had been exchanged.

"I hear you and Francesca gave Mrs F and Leah here a right good hiding last night, sir – I wish I could have been there instead of doing the boring rounds!"

"It was an enjoyable evening, certainly. From my point of view, though, it was especially useful in that it served to take my mind off the problems of this case. Anyway, I have a request. I need these letters delivered to my three officers, and to Mr & Mrs Harvey, and to Green, as soon as possible. You'll miss breakfast if I ask you to do this. Could you find a maid to take them round?"

"Of course, sir," said Alice, "but we'd better not use someone involved with breakfast. Leah, see if you can find Janet or Amy – they should be up in the dorms by now."

The girl immediately turned and disappeared up the staircase. She was back within a minute, with two uniformed maids following – not being quite so young and fit, they were some seconds behind.

"You want us to deliver some letters, sir?" asked the older woman, who was probably in her forties, but appeared to be the younger of the two.

"That's right. Sorry to interrupt your work. One to each of my officers in Somerville, Burdett-Coutts, and Wollstonecraft. One to Mrs Harvey in Pankhurst. One to the groundsman, Green, who could still be in his lodge – if not you'll have to hunt him down. I want you to put each envelope in the addressee's hand – don't just leave it with someone else. Understand?"

The two women nodded. "I'll take the one to Somerville and the one to Green, Amy," said the younger maid – "you do the other three."

They took the envelopes, and moved away.

"I'm sure you can work out what's in those envelopes?"

The two prefects grinned. "The ones to your men must contain orders, sir," suggested Alice.

"And the two others are setting up some more interviews," continued Leah.

"Quite correct. One day, in a hundred years, perhaps, humans will have learned how to communicate with each other by telepathy. Until then, I have to rely on written communications, or the telephone if I'm lucky.

"I assume you are back to the normal school routine today?"

"That's right, sir – Miss Armstrong sent round a note last night," confirmed Leah. "Can't say I'm sorry."

Miss Bennett arrived beside them, and immediately mentioned the previous evening's bridge. "Miss Fleming has told me what happened, Chief Inspector. She is keen to have some sort of revenge. If you are still with us tonight, she is proposing to set up two tables, and I'll be able to join you."

"Well, much as I'd like to say this case will be done and dusted today, I fear that it won't. So provisionally I'll be glad to accept the invitation."

The Housemistress joined them. "Good morning, Chief Inspector," she said with smile. "You look happy, and of course I concede that you have some justification for gloating. Now, Leah really is a good player, so if you can play again this evening, perhaps you will partner her for one rubber. I've put you on the second table for breakfast. Let's go in."

It was an adequate breakfast – Adair wasn't keen on porridge, and would have liked an extra sausage – but over the meal he had a pleasant discussion with a group of girls he hadn't spoken to before. Nobody mentioned the case, and nobody asked about detective work either. Instead, there was a discussion about the state of the world, especially in Europe, and about the likelihood of another war. The DCI was agreeably surprised at the level of understanding – and the amount of realism – demonstrated by girls of fifteen and sixteen. He reflected that these youngsters would almost inevitably come from homes where such things were talked about frequently, and this age group was old enough to sit at dinner with their educated parents and perhaps with equally erudite guests. He mentioned this point to his table, and heads nodded immediately.

"But it isn't as simple as that, sir," said Olivia, a little way down the table. "We get lessons – of a sort – here in school." Seeing Adair's surprise, she expanded on her statement.

"From the fifth form onwards, we all attend public affairs lessons – and talks from external people. Each term we have a series of visiting speakers. Politicians from all three major parties – and they aren't allowed to proselytise, but just talk in general terms from their different points of view. Senior civil servants – permanent secretaries, mainly. Senior officers from all three services. A top business man occasionally. Even a trade union leader. All those people back up what the Head teaches us about how the country works."

"That's right," confirmed Jemima sitting beside him. "We're taught a lot of things, sir, but perhaps the main thing is this – Miss Armstrong is always emphasising that we should listen to a variety of opinions before coming to a conclusion.

"Last week she actually said that while we must obey our parents, we shouldn't be afraid to politely question their beliefs and mores."

"Split infinitive, Jem," someone called along the table.

"Jemima will have to have some extra coaching from Miss Trelawney," the DCI suggested, and everyone laughed.

Adair knew that he would never be able to afford to send his own daughter to a school of this calibre, and even if he could he didn't think either he or his wife would ever allow her to leave home for weeks on end to be a boarder. He himself had received a very good education at a grammar school which had been founded some two hundred and fifty years before Willowbank, but he could see that this establishment was likely to outscore his old school in various ways. He wondered if any State school could ever provide this level of education.

Before the meal ended, he had fielded a tricky question on the merits versus the evils of gambling, and an even more tricky one on the question of capital punishment.

After breakfast, he returned to his room and collected his attaché case, before making his way back to the old part of the school. He found the Secretary reaching into a wooden four-drawer filing cabinet.

"Sorry, Chief Inspector, I'll be out of your way in just a minute," she said.

"Don't rush, Miss Spencer – it is your room, after all. Is Miss Armstrong free for a few minutes?"

"She has nobody with her at present – just go through."

Adair tapped on the interconnecting door, and went into the Head's spacious room.

"Good morning, Chief Inspector – did you have a good night?"

"Excellent, thank you ma'am – and the meals and the company were good too. I haven't seen my colleagues this morning as yet, but I'm sure they will also have been looked after very well.

"I've really come to ask two questions. First, is there another pupil who can read Arabic? I need one for ten minutes at most – and it's very urgent."

"Yes, apart from Aaliyah we have two others."

She paused as the Secretary came in with a word of apology and placed a folder in front of the Head.

"Angela, please find out where Leila Iqbal is this morning. Then apologise to whoever is teaching that class, and bring Leila back to Mr Adair."

"Perhaps Miss Spencer could also find out

where Miss Townsend is, and ask her to come and see me as early as possible during the morning break. I shouldn't keep her long."

Miss Spencer nodded, and left the room again. The Head looked enquiringly at the DCI.

"My second urgent need is to speak to Mr Hammadani. Ideally face-to-face, but by telephone if that isn't possible. Is he in the country, to your knowledge?"

"Not only is he in the country, but he'll be here in the school soon after lunch today. You may want to speak to him, but I have no doubt that he'll want to speak to you anyway!

"Will you have any progress to report to him?"

"Some, yes; I can't go into more detail just yet, but I'll give you an update later in the day.

"We'll be interviewing various people next door most of the morning – and incidentally I'll need to talk to Mr Dodds at some stage. My two sergeants will also be trying to see all the servants, but each interview will be only a two-minute job, and I've said that these can be carried out where each person is working. There should be minimum disruption."

"Yes, I understand. When you are ready for Bill, just tell him – he'll be here all day. If you want tea or coffee, just ask Angela. We have a kettle and so on in a little room just along the corridor."

Adair thanked the Headmistress, and returned to the next room. Here he found that all three of his men had arrived in his absence.

After the exchange of "good mornings", Adair enquired how his men's evening and night had gone. All three said the food had been nice, but there really wasn't enough of it for grown men. It seemed that the atmosphere in the public house's saloon bar was pleasant, but the beer was not kept as well as it should be. All three men had slept well.

"Right, that's the conventional pleasantries out of the way; let's get down to business. I assume you all got a note from me at breakfast time?"

The three men all nodded. "Good – I'll brief you all on what's happened. I assume you found nothing in your search, Inspector?"

"Nothing, sir."

"I didn't think there would be; I'll explain why in a minute. Anyway, Reynold's mugshot and prints have arrived from Essex." He slid the photograph over to Davison. Do you still think that he is Harvey?"

"More sure than ever, sir," replied the Inspector, after looking at the old picture.

"Very well. He and his supposed wife are coming in during the morning break. We'll wangle some prints off a cup or a piece of paper somehow. Incidentally, the original Mrs Reynolds is still alive, and confirms that she is still married to him.

"You've put the fingerprint kit in that room near the front door, Gemmill?"

"Yes, sir."

"Right. I have another printing job for you

in a minute, then you can go and join Borthwick talking to servants. But I want you to be back here by twenty-five past ten. The Harveys have been told to come and wait in that room as soon as the morning break starts. You will greet them, and apologise for the fact that there will be a slight delay as I'm running behind schedule. The Secretary will have put a jug of coffee in there – try and get them to sit down and take a cup. Don't force the issue, though. Understand?"

"Yes, sir."

"O.K. Now we come to the main bit of news. In Aaliyah's study, hidden inside a textbook on the bookshelf, I found this letter, dated last Saturday, and posted in London. It purports to be from her father. You can all read the detail when Gemmill has examined it for prints, but this is the gist of what it says.

"Aaliyah is told that her father is coming down on business – with Megan's father incidentally – on Monday. She is invited to inform Megan, and bring her to meet Mr Hammadani's driver outside. He will take them to a big hotel in the town, where the four of them will have dinner together. Because this outing is over and above the number of exeats allowed each term, the girl is enjoined to tell nobody other than Megan, because others would be jealous if they knew. Allegedly the Headmistress has approved the outing.

"Gemmill, take the letter to the other room, and get what prints you can. Then bring it back here and we'll have a quick discussion.

"While he's doing that, two other things should happen. Green is coming in to see us – should be here in about half an hour. Also, I have another Arabic-speaking pupil coming shortly – you'll soon see why."

Almost as he finished the sentence, there was a tap on the door, and Miss Spencer came in, followed by a girl of about seventeen, clearly of middle-eastern origin. Neither Adair nor Davison had seen her before, but Borthwick immediately smiled and said "hello, Leila."

"This is Leila Iqbal, sir – I sat next to her at breakfast this morning. Leila, this is Chief Inspector Adair and Inspector Davison." The girl smiled shyly, but said nothing as the DCI invited her to sit.

The Secretary was still hovering. "I passed your message to Miss Townsend, Chief Inspector. She actually has a free period before break time, but she'll come along a few minutes before ten-thirty."

"Thank you. Miss Spencer. One other task, if you please. Miss Armstrong says you have coffee-making facilities. At exactly half past ten, please place a jug of coffee, with milk and so on, and two cups, in the waiting room near the front door. That will be for Mr & Mrs Harvey, who may have to wait for a while.

"Understood. Shall I bring coffee in here for you as well?"

"Good idea – but a little earlier, perhaps – say ten-fifteen. Four cups, please, although I don't know if we'll need more than two."

The Secretary left, and Adair turned to the girl.

"I'm sorry to drag you away from your lesson, Leila, but I need your help in interpreting some writing."

"If this helps you to find Aaliyah, sir, I'll do anything. And you don't need to apologise for taking me away from an English Lit. lesson – I'm not very keen on Shakespeare anyway, and although *A Midsummer Night's Dream* is supposed to be a comedy I haven't come across a funny line yet."

The DCI grinned. "I recall thinking exactly the same thing about *A Comedy of Errors* when I was your age.

"Anyway, I want you to look at a few letters, and interpret some Arabic for me."

He pushed the three older letters across the table, and Leila unfolded the first and started to read. After a few seconds she stopped, and looked up.

"Although this is typed, it's a private letter from Aaliyah's father – should I be seeing this?"

"Given the circumstances, it's essential, and in a few minutes you'll see why. Actually, I am quite sure that both Mr Hammadani and his daughter would approve of what I'm asking you to do.

"In fact, the main content of these three letters isn't important – although the style may be. And it's the short piece of Arabic that I want you to translate."

Leila bent her head to continue reading. She then read the remaining two letters.

"The sections in Arabic are either short statements or instructions, sir. One says 'work hard at your mathematics'. Another says 'your results in the history test are most pleasing'. The third says 'your Mother and I know you will go on to great things'. Since those could have been included within the typed English text, I guess he just included them to give Leila a bit of practice in Arabic."

"Very likely. Now, Leila, I'm going to let you into a secret. I'd like you to keep this entirely to yourself for the time being – do you understand?

"Of course, sir. You can trust me completely."

"Good. Aaliyah received another letter, on the morning she disappeared. It also appears to be from her father, and it explains why she left the school grounds – and why Lady Megan went with her. But we think the author of the letter forged it to appear like the three you have just read. We are just testing the new letter for fingerprints – come along and read it. Come as well, you two."

The girl was staring at the DCI in horror as he spoke, but she stood up, and joined Adair as he left the room. The other officers followed.

They trooped into the waiting room, where Sergeant Gemmill was sitting at the table, making notes in his pocket book. The letter and envelope were on the table, and a camera was laying nearby.

Gemmill jumped up as the others entered the room.

"Finished, Sergeant?" enquired Adair.

"Yes, sir, just a mish-mash on the envelope, but some decent ones on the letter. Some must be the poor girl's, and if the others belong to the writer then all I can say is that he – or she – doesn't much care about being identified."

"Yes – we'll come back to that point. This is Leila, Sergeant; she is going to interpret the bit in Arabic. Blow the worst of the powder off, please, then cover the first part of the letter so Leila can just see the Arabic at this stage."

Gemmill nodded, and did exactly as his boss had instructed. He folded the letter so that only the very last bit was showing, and beckoned the girl forward.

She only took a few seconds to look at the script, and turned to Adair.

"It just says 'I'm very proud of you'."

"Thank you. Now, is there any difference between that writing and that on the other three letters?"

The four officers waited in silence while the girl scrutinised the Arabic in all four letters. A minute later she looked up again.

"I don't know. Mr Hammadani presumably

dictated these letters to a secretary to be typed. My first assumption was that he added the Arabic line when he signed the letters, but now I don't think that can be so. I can't be sure, but it looks as though at least three different people wrote the Arabic lines. Two of the first three look to have the same handwriting, but one is different. The last one is different again. So I am guessing that Mr Hammadani dictated the extra bit, and told whichever secretary it was to hand write that in Arabic. He's a very important man, and will have several secretaries, I think."

There was a silence for a moment, as the detectives took in what the girl had said. Then Adair stirred. "Thank you, Leila – most helpful. Please unfold the last letter now, and read it. I'm sorry you'll get a bit messy from the fingerprint powder."

It didn't take long for the girl to read the fourth letter, and in a matter of seconds she pushed it aside and looked up again.

"That's awful, sir. It can't have been Mr Hammadani who wrote this, surely? Just to kidnap Megan?"

"Very unlikely, but it can't be ruled out yet. Just one final thing, Leila. Suppose you had received such a letter would you be suspicious? Or would you just jump for joy at the thought of getting away from school for an evening?"

The girl considered the question.

"Well, sir, I'm probably three years older

than Aaliyah. Now, I'd think the suggestion was very odd. But when I was her age, I don't suppose I would have thought twice. I think I'd have done exactly as I was instructed."

Adair thanked Leila warmly, and sent her back to her boring lesson.

"Inspector, Sergeant, you two haven't had a chance to read that last letter yet. Have a quick look now."

Both did so. Adair then led the team back to the office, telling Gemmill to collect up all the letters and bring them with him.

"All right. Any observations, gentlemen?"

"Could that last one be by Aaliyah's father, sir? As Leila suggested, so he could kidnap Megan and get a hefty ransom for her?"

"Well, as I said to her, we can't rule it out, Borthwick. But it seems very improbable. For a start, the man is immensely rich already. And he is due to arrive here sometime today. I can't think he'd turn up if he's guilty."

"The business of the prints, sir," said Davison. If – and I know it's a big if – they are the writer's, then they don't care. That must be significant, surely?"

"Perhaps. It could be that the writer, having told Aaliyah to destroy the letter, assumed that she would do so. Or maybe, having got a very large sum of money, the writer intends to leave England and settle in one of those countries which have no extradition treaty with us – there are a few in

South America, I think.

"Anyway, we now know why the girls went to meet someone. We still have no idea who. And as we now know that Aaliyah was told to leave the school by a back door and go round to the swimming pool, we can assume that this 'driver' didn't park his car out at the front as one would have expected. In fact, I think he must have entered and left the school via the rear drive, where the chances of being seen would be very slim. What conclusion can we draw from that?"

"That he wasn't a stranger here, sir?" suggested Davison.

"That's right. It would seem that he knew this place very well.

"All right. Gemmill, Borthwick, you make a start talking to the servants. Come back to do your coffee thing as we've discussed, Gemmill. If Mr Harvey does drink coffee, when he leaves to come in here, get busy with checking the cup and saucer. Take this envelope with the Essex prints. If there's a match, stick your head in the door here and give a meaningful nod. Got it?"

"Yes sir."

Right – you two carry on. Green should be here in a minute, but I've got another job for Miss Spencer. Wait here a second."

Adair got up and went out via the corridor to find the Secretary in the Bursar's room. Apologising to Dodds for interrupting, the DCI addressed Miss Spencer.

"Can you please find me the telephone number for the Earl of Trimley? I need to speak to him."

"I have the lists here, Chief inspector – one moment."

She riffled though some papers, and then jotted the number down on a notepad. Tearing off the top sheet, she handed it to the DCI.

Thanks. By the way, Mr Dodds, I'd like a few minutes with you later this morning – routine, as you'll appreciate."

"Of course, Chief Inspector, whenever you want."

CHAPTER 10

Adair arrived back at the office door just as Green arrived. The DCI introduced Davison and himself, and invited the groundsman to take a seat. The man looked very wary.

"You know why we're here, Green?"

Yes, sir – the two girls."

"Do you know anything about their disappearance?"

"No, 'course not."

"Where were you, day before yesterday, between four and five?"

I'd been putting lines on the hockey pitches, sir. When it got dusk – and I s'pose that'd be about four – I took the white line machine into the shed, and started to do some maintenance on the gang mower. I was in the shed until knocking off time at half five."

"Anyone see you in there?"

"No, but Mr Painter knew that's where I was; it was him who told me to go and work on the mowers."

"How far is your shed from the swimming

pool?"

Green stared. "I don't know; two or three hundred yards, I suppose. It's right away from the school buildings."

Did you see any car at that time, perhaps using the rear drive towards your lodge?"

The man shook his head. The shed isn't near that drive either, sir. I didn't see – or hear – any cars."

"You have a motor cycle, I understand," continued Adair. There are sidecars which could carry two young girls – do you have such a thing?"

"I don't, sir, no. My bike is only a little thing – no way does it take a sidecar."

"Very well. Just one other thing. When you applied for the job here, did you tell them that you had been in prison for theft?"

Green looked as though he was about to burst into tears.

"No sir, I didn't," he admitted. "I wanted the job, and knew I'd not stand much chance if they heard I'd been inside. I was afraid this would come out – I knew you were bound to look at everyone's record. I made a stupid mistake, and paid for it. But I've not put a foot wrong since I got out. I suppose I'll be sacked now. Oh God."

"I don't think you'll lose the job, Green. I've spoken to the headmistress. Off you go, and keep working hard."

"Thank you very much, sir; that's a great relief to me!"

"Did you get any sense that he might have been involved in the abduction?" asked the DCI when the groundsman had gone.

"None at all," replied Davison. "I got the impression he really likes working here. And, as he said, he paid for his mistake and seems to deserve his new chance."

"Yes, that's what I think. Excuse me a minute – I'm going to see if I can talk to Megan's father.

He wondered whether the Head would be using the telephone, but on picking up the handset he heard nothing but the hum of an open line until the operator cut in to ask what number he wanted. He gave the number Miss Spencer had written down for him. The operator told him to hang up, and she would call him back when she could make the long-distance connection.

"There's something that's bothering me about this, Davison, but I can't put my finger on it. Anyway, I'm convinced that this 'driver' must be very familiar with the layout here – the roads and the buildings. Or at least that the instigator – if that's a different person – described in detail where the driver should go."

He shook his head, baffled.

"The Hammadani girl had to make contact with Megan sometime between when she read the letter during the morning break and – presumably – the end of the lunch break," remarked Davison. "Given they aren't in the same house, she must have done that in school. We could make enquiries as to whether anyone saw them talking?"

"Yes, I agree they must have spoken, but I don't think anything hinges on where or when."

The two sat in silence for a minute, each lost in his own thoughts.

"Well, sir, we don't have many car-owning insiders. Miss Townsend, Mr & Mrs Harvey, Mr Dodds, and Doctor & Mrs Livermore. Although I suppose a car could have been hired."

"That's a very good point. Look into that later, will you? The local nick can probably help with names of car-hire people."

The telephone rang, and Adair picked it up immediately. He identified himself, and then said "I see, thank you...Please tell his lordship that I don't have any specific news about his daughter – I just have a question...Yes...Thanks again."

Replacing the receiver, he looked at his colleague. "Lord Trimley is out with his agent, visiting some farm on the estate. He's expected back in an hour or so, and the secretary will ask him to call. In the meantime, we'll talk to Dodds."

Davison started to get up, but the DCI waved him down. "No, I'll go and fetch him."

He returned within a minute, accompanied by Dodds.

"Take a pew, Mr Dodds," invited Adair. "As I'm sure you appreciate, we think this crime has been committed by – or at least with the assistance of – an insider. Also, some sort of motor vehicle must have been used. So, obviously, we're looking at members of staff with cars.

"Tell us, please, what you were doing between four o'clock and six o'clock on Monday afternoon."

"I was in my office most of the afternoon, Chief Inspector, except for a few minutes when I went into the Head's room, and even fewer minutes when I probably visited the lavatory. As it happened, I was with the Head at about ten minutes past four, because the first teachers arrived for the four-fifteen staff meeting while I was with her. I left then, and returned to my own office. I should explain that I attend what Lucy calls the 'senior staff meeting' – that's her, Eleanor Livermore, me, and the Chairman of Governors – but Monday's meeting was for teaching staff only.

"Anyway, I was in my office from about four-fifteen until about ten to six. And before you ask, no, I have no witness to that. Nobody came to see me – apart from Lucy, Eleanor and Angela, hardly anyone ever does. Angela would have been in the meeting – she does the minutes and so on. Nor, as far as I remember, did I make or receive any telephone calls."

"Obviously the absence of an alibi doesn't presume guilt, Mr Dodds; it just makes it harder to eliminate people from our enquiries. What time did you get home – and do you have a family?"

"It takes me between fifteen and twenty minutes to drive home, so I suppose I arrived about six-fifteen. I have a wife – my two children have flown the nest."

"Where do you park your car while you're working?" asked Davison.

"By the main front entrance, Inspector. There's plenty of room. The only time I park it around the back out of sight is when there is a function of some sort – Speech Day, for example – and lots of parents are coming. My ancient Redwing is a bit out of place among the big expensive cars!"

Both policemen had noticed the car when they first arrived, and each man had admired it from the other side of the car park.

"I'd say its status is as high as any car, Mr Dodds, and much appreciated by people. I was talking to one of the third-year girls yesterday, and she said she'd love to go for a ride in it – in the summer. And if memory serves, this was originally a very expensive vehicle – about five hundred pounds new in 1922?"

"Quite correct, Chief Inspector. My father bought this one new in 1923. He died unexpectedly in 1928, and I inherited it. I couldn't afford five hundred pounds now, let alone back in 1923!

"But if your reference to the youngster wanting a ride in it is meant to imply that I could have picked up the two missing girls, you're off target. Redwings do come in four-seat form, but mine is only a two-seater. It's quite correct that travelling in it is best in summer, though. In winter it's cold and draughty!"

The two officers smiled, each having decided that the Bursar was not the abductor.

"Many thanks, Mr Dodds," said Adair. "Hopefully we won't need to trouble you again."

After the man left, there was another silence, until the DCI spoke again.

"I didn't say this in front of Borthwick and Gemmill, but I have to admit that it was a chance remark by a child over dinner last night which made me kick myself and go and do a thorough search of Aaliyah's study – something I should have organised at the outset.

"Now there's something else that is so obvious that I should have seen it earlier too. The letters. If that fourth letter is indeed a very clever forgery, then someone got hold of one or more of the earlier ones. Assuming the girl didn't leave her father's correspondence lying around in the main part of the school, that means someone with access to her study. I have to say that the Housemistress and House Tutor in Lovelace are really nice ladies – and of course both were present in the staff meeting on Monday anyway."

"Not just a glance at the other letters either, sir. To make a copy, you'd surely need at least one original in front of you. Looks like one of Aaliyah's school friends must have been involved."

"Yes, I agree that a letter must have been taken away to copy. I guess the assumption was that one letter probably wouldn't be missed – and

Aaliyah wouldn't worry about it even if she did notice. Or, I suppose, the purloined copy could have been returned later. If a child is involved, this is going to get even trickier."

The DCI was about to add something more when the telephone rang again. He picked up the handset again.

"DCI Adair here. Oh, yes m'lord... News of a sort, yes... We know how the girls were persuaded to leave the building.... Yes...No, not yet...Miss Hammadani received a letter, apparently from her father, saying that he was involved in business discussions with you, and that you and he would take your respective daughters out to dinner on Monday. Aaliyah Hammadani was told to inform Lady Megan, but the whole thing was to be kept secret...No, m'lord...No, we don't...Well, you've already answered the question I was going to ask, and that was about any business connection you may have with Mr Hammadani...I see, yes...It's a matter for you, m'lord, but I don't think it could help...thank you...Goodbye."

Replacing the receiver, Adair looked at his Inspector.

"As you probably gathered, Lord Trimley has had no business dealings with Hammadani. The two men have met here on various occasions, and like each other. But, as Trimley explained, Hammadani is an international businessman, where he himself just runs an estate – and much of that work is done by an agent. The two have no business interests in common.

"Trimley says he made enquiries about me personally, and decided he wouldn't keep piling on pressure – which is why the Yard hasn't been plagued by him in the same way that it apparently has by some of the unaffected parents. I guess Hammadani is the same. Trimley asked if there was any point in his coming down here, but there isn't, of course."

Adair sat looking morose, when the telephone rang. Picking up the handset, he found to his surprise that it was Lord Trimley again. The tone of this conversation was different, and Davison could hear the distant caller's voice, although he still couldn't pick out the words.

"What?...Right...Would you repeat that, m'lord...Yes...Yes, certainly...I could ask someone from the Suffolk police to bring it...Very well, thank you very much...Yes...Yes, I'll tell her at once...No, we won't...Very well...I'll see you later."

"Things are moving, Davison. Trimley has just received a ransom demand. Fifty thousand pounds, to be paid into one of those Swiss numbered bank accounts. Failing to pay by five o'clock on Friday afternoon will mean Megan's whereabouts will not be divulged, and she will eventually die of starvation. There is no mention of Aaliyah. The letter emphasises that the police are not to be involved. The Earl is bringing the letter to us here – he says he has a fast car, and even though the roads up his way aren't too good he estimates he'll be here in four hours.

There was a tap on the door, and Miss Spencer came in, followed by a maid carrying a tray.

"Your coffee, gentlemen. We'll deliver to the waiting room in a few minutes."

The two women left, and Adair stood up. Pour the coffee," he instructed, I must just brief Miss Armstrong."

Once again he tapped on the communicating door and went into the Head's room.

"News of a sort, ma'am," he said, after being waved to a chair.

"Minutes ago, Lord Trimley received a ransom demand – fifty thousand pounds for the safe return of his daughter. He is bringing the letter here himself. I emphasise that this is absolutely secret for the moment. The demand specifies that the police are not to be involved – it's to his lordship's credit that he has ignored that, but obviously the fact that he has must be kept completely secret. Please don't mention this to a single soul – we now know that someone within the school is definitely involved."

"I understand. But fifty thousand pounds..."

"Yes. The mind boggles – and of course if that demand is duplicated for Aaliyah...

"Anyway, I can't go into detail, but we know where the girls left the building, and what caused them to do so. But as yet we don't know who – and it must be more than one person – was involved. However, we're narrowing the field, as it were. I expect Mr Hammadani to be able to help us on a point when he arrives.

"Does he have a house and office in London, ma'am?"

"Both, I understand. He flew in today on the Imperial Airways flight from Cairo. How he got there I really don't know. He was in London on Monday evening, and I understood he was about to go to Beirut." Miss Armstrong shook her head in bewilderment. "Anyway, this morning he telephoned from Croydon, and said he was going into his office before driving down here."

"So that means he probably won't call at his London house. A pity, as I guess he'll have a letter from the kidnapper waiting there. Can't be helped. If you'll excuse me, ma'am, I must carry on."

The DCI returned to the office, and almost abstractedly began to sip at his coffee. Within a minute, there was a knock on the door, and a young woman put her head inside.

"I'm Felicity Townsend – Angela Spencer said you wanted to see me?"

"Yes, please come in, Miss Townsend, said Adair, as he and Davison rose to their feet. "This is Inspector Davison, and I'm Chief Inspector Adair. Do sit down. We have fresh coffee here – would you care for a cup?"

"Yes please. I would normally have one in the staff room at this time. White, no sugar, please."

Miss Townsend looked to be about twenty-five, with brown hair and horn-rimmed spectacles. She wore a nondescript cardigan, cream blouse, and long skirt. She was displaying no jewellery of any kind. Both officers privately thought she was dressed and made up to look less attractive than she really was. Neither said anything, but the woman divined their thoughts.

"I'm the youngest teacher here by quite a margin," she remarked. "I think it is politically advisable not to flaunt that fact. I don't say that any of my spinster colleagues here would show or even feel jealousy, but after university I taught elsewhere for a year, and I certainly experienced that in my previous school."

Both detectives nodded understandingly.

"I imagine you can alter that image very effectively when appropriate," said Adair. "But it's only the matter of your alibi that we are interested in. Please talk us through what happened from the end of your last lesson on Monday, up to say six p.m."

"Yes, of course. It's quite straightforward. I should have attended the routine staff meeting in Lucy's office at a quarter past four. But my mother was quite poorly, and I wanted to get back to her as soon as possible. I spoke to Lucy earlier in the day, and she gave her blessing for me to skip the meeting.

"So, at about five past four, I suppose, I

got into my car and drove home. The journey typically takes fifteen minutes, so I would have been indoors by four-twenty or thereabouts. I saw no girls outside the building as I went to the car, and no other car either – except for Bill's sports car, which was parked next to mine as usual. Oh, and Brian Redpath's was parked there too, for some reason.

"Mother and I have no telephone, gentlemen. I knew nothing of what had happened until I arrived in school the next morning – when I found all the girls confined to their houses, and all lessons cancelled. Quite a shock, I can tell you."

"I'm sure it must have been, Miss Townsend. So if we were to speak to your mother, she could vouch for the time you say you got home?"

"She certainly could, and she would also tell you that I didn't bring two hostages with me, and lock them in the garden shed. Although I expect you'd be a bit cynical about her testimony!"

"Quite right, miss," replied Davison, "but even if true it wouldn't completely exonerate you. You might have brought the two girls away from school, and before reaching home handed them over to an accomplice. You'd have had time to do that, I think."

"I suppose that's so, Inspector. Well, all I can say is that I didn't. What's apparently happening to these two must be extremely frightening for them. I hope that at least they're together and able to support each other. And, of course, that they aren't being harmed in any way."

"Amen to that," said the DCI. "Is there anything else which you think might have any bearing on this matter?"

"Not really," replied the young lady. "I don't teach either of the girls this year, as it happens, although last year I taught both. All I'd say is that I didn't realise they were friends – I know they aren't in the same house, and I don't remember ever seeing them together around the school. So I'm surprised they've disappeared as a couple, so to speak."

"That's all right, Miss Townsend; we have a pretty good idea as to how and why that happened. Thank you for coming across to see us."

CHAPTER 11

"Right," said Adair when the teacher had gone. "It's ten to eleven. Nip along and collect the Harveys – assuming they've turned up.

Two minutes later, the Harveys entered the room, and introductions were effected.

"I'm so sorry to keep you both waiting," the DCI apologised, "and I realise that you need to get back in a few minutes to start another lesson, ma'am. So we'll start with you – it won't take long in your case.

"Let me get this right. On Monday, you attended a staff meeting in Miss Armstrong's room at four-fifteen?"

"That's right. The meeting went on until a little after half past five."

"Yes. And although you have a car, only Mr Harvey can drive?"

"Again, correct."

"Thank you. I don't need to ask you any more questions – you're free to get back to your classroom."

"I think I prefer to stay, Chief Inspector, if

you're going to accuse my husband of abducting the girls."

"As you wish. Mr Harvey, where were you between four p.m. and six p.m. on Monday?"

"I had gone into town immediately after lunch. I parked behind the Blue Angel. I had an appointment with my tailor – the first fitting for a new suit. Babcock will vouch for my presence. That was at half past two. Next, I looked in a couple of bookshops, and browsed in them for a while. Then I walked along the high street, looking in shoe shop windows for perhaps half an hour. Then, I drove back here. I suppose I got back to the house at about five o'clock."

"Did you speak to anyone or even see anyone when you arrived back – a maid, or a child?" enquired Adair.

"I don't think so. I parked at the back of the house, and entered by the back door, straight into our private quarters."

Inspector Davison took up the questioning. "In the town, how long did your fitting take?"

"I suppose about twenty minutes."

"I see. And did you speak to anyone in either bookshop?"

"No. There were a few other customers browsing like I was. I didn't speak to any of them – we didn't take any notice of each other, actually. And I didn't speak to an assistant in either shop. In both cases the assistant was sitting behind a counter reading a book and taking no notice of customers. I suppose they'd have paid attention if someone had wanted to buy anything."

"And the shoe shops. Did you actually go into any of those?"

"No; just window shopping."

The door behind the Harveys opened silently, and Gemmill gave a 'thumbs up' signal before reclosing the door equally silently.

The DCI spoke again. "So, it amounts to this. You can show where you were until about ten minutes to three. After that time, we only have your word for it as to where you went – and what time you came home. Basically, you don't have an alibi.

"Now, we know the two girls were driven away from here in a car. For reasons which I can't go into, there is no doubt whatsoever that someone from the school was involved – probably more than one person. Not many people here have cars, and we have already been able to eliminate most of the others.

"Would you like to comment?"

"I should, Chief Inspector," interjected Mrs Harvey, looking indignant. "To suggest Jonathan would kidnap these girls is just ludicrous. Where do you think he could have taken them? He would never do anything wrong."

"That's an interesting statement, ma'am. Let's examine it a little more closely. Did your name used to be Reynolds, Mr Harvey?"

Both Davison and Adair thought the man

stiffened very slightly, but he was calm enough when he replied.

Certainly not. I can't imagine why you ask me that."

"Well," continued the DCI, "in 1924 or thereabouts, a young man appeared at the Essex Assizes. His name was Reynolds, and he was convicted – actually he pleaded guilty – to a charge of bigamy. He was sent to prison for three and a half years. Does that mean anything to you, Mr Harvey?"

"Nothing," replied the man tersely.

"That's rather surprising," said Adair, "considering your fingerprints and those of Reynolds match."

The man slumped into his chair.

"I'm sorry, ma'am. Not only did this man serve time for bigamy, but his first wife is still very much alive, and is still legally married to him. I'm afraid you must revert to being Miss Ross.

"Reynolds, normally local officers carry out arrests, but we don't have any present so we'll abandon the conventions. I'm arresting you on suspicion of bigamy. At the station you'll be charged with an offence under the Offences Against the Person Act 1861. The Act provides for a sentence of up to seven years – and for a second offence I think you can safely anticipate receiving the maximum.

"I don't actually think you are the kidnapper – but if you are I suggest you say so very quickly, before any harm comes to the girls.

"Inspector, call Mr Hatrick at the station, and ask him to send a couple of men to take Reynolds away. Then fetch Gemmill from the waiting room, if he's still there. He can look after the man until the locals arrive.

Davison picked up the telephone.

While he was speaking to the police station, Reynolds sat staring at the floor. His 'wife' who appeared to be red with anger, but with tears in her eyes, spoke.

"I suppose I should have realised. Everything was just too good to be true. Well, this is utterly humiliating for me, but I expect I'll get over it eventually. What will sustain me is the thought of you rotting away in prison. I hope it's an early taste of hell, because that's where you'll go eventually."

Reynolds made no reply. He didn't even look at her. She rose, nodded to the DCI, and walked out of the room just as Davison returned with Gemmill.

"Take Reynolds to the waiting room, Sergeant, and look after him until the locals arrive. Better put him in handcuffs."

"Do you think he's the kidnapper, Inspector?" asked the DCI when the others had gone.

"In all honesty, no sir."

"Nor do I. It's nearly time for lunch, but I must just give Miss Armstrong the news about

Reynolds. If you see Gemmill and Borthwick, tell them we'll meet here again at half past one."

Adair tapped on the Head's door, and found her on the telephone. She waved him to a seat. From the half of the conversation he could hear, it was clear that there was an upset parent on the line. After two minutes, Mrs Armstrong replaced the receiver.

"He's taking his daughter out of the school. I can't blame the man, but that's the fifth. Yes, the children may come back, but who knows?

"From the expression on your face, you're not bringing me good news."

"No ma'am. I've just arrested Mr Harvey – but for bigamy, nothing to do with the abductions. Miss Ross is just a little upset. But, as she told him he could rot in prison prior to spending an eternity in hell, I think she realises that she is well out of it."

"Oh, Lord. This is what you meant earlier about a 'delicate matter'?"

"Yes."

"I'll go and talk to her. She'll need a few days off. Any other news?"

"Alas no, ma'am."

***

Adair walked across to Lovelace House, where a dozen or more girls were standing around in the hallway, talking. In the buzz of conversation, he thought he detected a different atmosphere. Seeing Alice talking to a couple of other girls, he went to join them.

"Good afternoon Alice, Fenella, Evelyn."

"Very good, sir," said Alice. I reckon I have a good memory, but to remember the names of these two after meeting so many others in the last day or so is impressive, to say the least."

"Well, as I said to these two yesterday, I'll forget their names again soon. One has to – my brain has a finite capacity, and I'll soon need to take in new names, and lots of other new details.

"Is it my imagination, or is there something going on?"

Alice laughed. "In a way. We've just been told that there's to be a house inspection at half past four today. Everyone, from Miss Fleming down, tends to be a bit on edge. Especially the staff, actually."

"Oh, I see. The Headmistress comes in from time to time to see everything in the house is hunky dory?"

"Not the Head, no – the Deputy Head. Although the Head inspects the Deputy's house – and is equally sharp, allegedly. Many years ago, it seems the then Governors made a rule that says that each house is to be formally inspected once in each term – with a maximum of four hours' notice being given. There should also be several less formal inspections – at least one every half-term."

"What happens at these inspections?"

"We don't see everything, of course. But for the formal inspection Mrs Livermore probably goes into most rooms in the house – common rooms, studies, dining room, changing rooms, kitchen, etc., and spends over two hours here. She certainly looks for dirt and so on – last time I actually saw her running her finger along the top of the dining room door. She talks to various people as she goes round – pupils and staff. I've seen her giving a housemaid almost third-degree treatment. She becomes a different person when she has her inspector's hat on."

"What about the informal inspections?" asked Adair, who was experiencing a sudden sense of enlightenment. This time Evelyn replied.

"Oh, she comes in and wanders around when she feels like it. Nobody knows she's coming, not even Miss Fleming. People have seen her occasionally, and she speaks to anyone she happens to see – asks how they're getting on, that sort of thing."

"Normally, each housemistress is supreme in her own house, you see," explained Alice. But Mrs Livermore can override her at any time she chooses. We girls don't much mind the formal inspections – it mostly just means a rapid bit of tidying up. But I think the staff get a little stressed!"

"Here comes Miss F," muttered Fenella. "Time to go in."

In the dining room, Adair found himself on the one table he had not yet sat on. He was just learning the girls' names when the Housemistress came across and spoke.

"You may have heard that I'm a bit tied up this afternoon, Chief Inspector. I fear I must leave lunch early – my apologies to you."

"I'm in the same position, ma'am and I too will have to leave after the first course. I'm sorry, everyone," he said to the disappointed-looking girls who had heard his remark. "I expect to be back tonight and tomorrow, so perhaps I can sit with you again."

"Certainly," said Miss Fleming; "I'll arrange that – and I'm really looking forward to the bridge!"

Adair was preoccupied over the first course, and apologised profusely to his table as he rose to leave. "I'm a bit distracted by something that's happening, but I'll endeavour to concentrate when we sit down again tonight."

He walked back to his office, where he immediately picked up the telephone and asked the operator to put him through to Dr Livermore's practice in the town. Within a minute, the telephone was answered.

"Livermore and Graves, good afternoon."

"I'd like to speak to Dr Livermore, urgently. This is Detective Chief Inspector Adair, of Scotland Yard."

"Oh dear – he isn't here right now, and I'm only the Receptionist. We're closed for lunch, but I think I'd better fetch his partner, Dr Graves, who's in his surgery."

There was a 'clunk' as the woman put down the receiver. After nearly two minutes, it was picked up again, and a deep voice said "Graves here. This is presumably about the missing girls?"

"Yes, Doctor. I need to speak to your partner, as a matter of urgency."

"Well, assuming you're at the school, at present he's nearer to you than to me. His wife called me on Monday, and said he was sick – influenza, she said. Told me I'd have to hold the fort for a few days. If you want to talk to him he'll be in bed in his house, nursed by Eleanor, no doubt."

The DCI paused for a moment to consider. Then, making up his mind, he spoke again.

"No, Doctor, you're wrong. Dr Livermore left the marital home over the weekend. He isn't in the school. Would you have any idea where else he might be staying?"

"Oh Lord. No. Oh, wait; perhaps I do. Before he married Eleanor – must be about two years ago now – he used to live in an old farmhouse up on the Kent Downs. I suppose it's possible he never sold the place."

"What's the address, Doctor?"

"God knows. I went there a few times, but can't recall the actual address. Wait a second – Miriam here will have it."

After a brief pause during which Adair could hear pages in some sort of record book being turned, the Doctor came back.

"Got it, Chief Inspector. Forty Acre Farm, Wealden Road, Lyminge. But neither of us knows if Keith still owns the place."

"Understood. I'd appreciate it if you say nothing to anybody, Doctor – and ask your Receptionist to say silent too."

"Of course, Chief Inspector. Rely on it."

Adair juggled the receiver rest until the operator came back on the line. "Get me the police station, please."

When the station answered, the DCI identified himself, and asked for either Inspector Hatrick or the Superintendent. Within seconds, Hatrick was on the line.

"Thanks for sending us the bigamist, sir – he's been formally charged. How can I help you now?"

Does your local magistrates' court sit today?"

No, sir, but it does tomorrow."

"All right – in that case I need the name of a magistrate I can approach at home or at work – I need a search warrant urgently."

"Nearest to you is Mr Mills, sir – Oakleigh House. Turn right at the main gate of the school, and it's a big house about half a mile along on the left-hand side. Can't miss it, really. Mr Mills is an experienced man. Hang on – I've got a telephone number here somewhere."

Seconds later, Hatrick produced the number.

"One other thing, Inspector. Can you rustle up three or four uniformed officers for me, if we need to carry out a raid?"

"Certainly – I'll come myself with some men. Shall we join you now?"

"Wait a bit – I'll have to get the warrant sorted first. But does your set of six-inch maps extend to Lyminge?"

"I think so, sir, yes."

"Good. Please bring that sheet with you when you come to the school. I'll get back to you shortly."

Once again Adair jiggled the receiver. He gave the number which Hatrick had just provided, and after first speaking to Mrs Mills her husband came on the line. The DCI explained the situation briefly, and the Magistrate agreed to hear an application. Adair said he would send someone as soon as possible.

Putting down the telephone, he started to write on a convenient foolscap pad. He had just finished this task, when all three of his subordinates returned.

"Right, gentlemen, progress – I hope."

He rapidly outlined what he had learned.

"Inspector, take this information I've drafted, and go and swear it before the magistrate chap, Mills. He's expecting you. Request a warrant to enter and search this Forty Acre Farm." He described how to find the Magistrate's house.

"If he refuses to issue a warrant, we'll have

to think again.

"Gemmill, Borthwick, go and find Mrs Livermore in her house. I'll take a risk. On my authority, arrest her on suspicion of being an accessory before the fact to an act of kidnapping, caution her, and bring her in here."

Yes sir," replied Borthwick. "I've never come across a case – what's the law on that?"

"It's a Common Law offence, like murder. Go."

Once again, Adair went through to speak to the Head.

"More bad news, Chief Inspector? The business with Harvey or whatever his name is won't do the school's reputation any good."

"I'm afraid there is far worse, ma'am. I have just sent officers to arrest your Deputy on suspicion of being an accessory to kidnapping. I'm also seeking a warrant to enter premises which we believe belongs to her husband."

For the first time he saw the woman look shocked. He paused.

Mrs Armstrong was now very pale. "You expect to find the girls at this place?"

"I certainly hope so. If I've got this wrong I'm going to be in very deep trouble."

The Head was silent for a moment.

"I can't come to terms with all this, Chief Inspector. When can I speak to the Chairman of Governors?"

"If you could wait a couple of hours or so,

ma'am, we should have definite news. Now, just one more thing. I'd like to borrow two of your teachers as soon as possible. I want them to accompany police officers – so if we find Megan and Aaliyah they can be with familiar females. One from Lovelace and one from Wollstonecraft, if possible."

"Yes, of course. Just a moment – I'll fetch Angela."

The Head rose from her chair and went out to the Bursar's office. She returned within a minute.

"Angela is just checking the timetables to see where Jackie Bennett and Laura Filby are at present. I think it would be better to use the House Tutors – they're nearer the girls' age than the Housemistresses."

Adair had no time to comment, as the Secretary came in.

"Jackie has a tutorial in the library, Lucy, and no other lesson this afternoon. Laura is in Room 17 with a fourth-year history class. After that she'll be in the same room with a first-year class."

"Excellent. Go to the library, please, and ask Jackie to come to your office at once. Her girls can stay and read. She'll find out why when she arrives – neither of you should speculate. I'll go and take over Laura's classes, and send her over here too."

"Thank you ma'am," said the DCI, "I must get on."

His return to the Secretary's office coincided

with the arrival of Mrs Livermore and the two sergeants. The expression in the woman's face was one of fury, but Adair thought he could detect fear as well. She said nothing as he waved her to a chair. Gemmill spoke first.

"Sir, you should know that when we entered the private quarters, we found several suitcases in the process of being packed. Two in the bedroom, and two more in the living room."

"How interesting. Funny time to be going on holiday, Mrs Livermore – there are still several weeks of the school term remaining. Have you been given leave of absence?"

The Deputy just stared at the table, and made no reply.

"Where is your husband?"

Again there was no response.

"Very well – I'm not going to waste time with you. Take her to the waiting room, Borthwick, and stay with her. Make a note of anything she says. But note this well, Mrs Livermore. If the girls have been harmed in any way, you are equally responsible, and will be punished accordingly. If – heaven forbid – they are dead, you'll hang."

The woman seemed to be about to speak, but then rose and left the room meekly with the Sergeant.

Gemmill and Adair sat in silence for a few minutes. Then the door burst open, and Davison came in.

"Got it, sir," he said, smiling, and brandishing a paper.

"Excellent." Adair picked up the telephone, and asked for the police station again.

When he reached Inspector Hatrick, he just said "Can you come up to the school right away? Good.

"He's got the men already sitting in two cars, and they'll be with us in ten minutes. Did you have any trouble getting the warrant, Inspector?"

"Well, the Magistrate asked a few questions. One was about how we knew the farm was still owned by Livermore. I had to admit that we didn't – just said time was of the essence, that sort of thing. I thought he was going to refuse, but he signed the warrant. As he pushed it across the table to me he said this, in these words, as far as I can remember. 'I don't think I can issue a warrant with formal conditions on it. But I'll say this orally. If when you arrive, the occupier says that he bought the place off Livermore, then I trust that you won't attempt to execute it.' I thought that was fair enough, sir, and so I agreed."

"Yes, indeed. Right. Two car loads of our uniformed colleagues will arrive in a moment. Also we're borrowing two teachers who'll come on the raid with us. Not sure what we're going to do with Mrs Livermore – I don't know if you saw her in the corridor as you came in, Inspector, but she's in the waiting room with Borthwick, under arrest.

Davison only had time to say "Good", when a

knock on the door presaged the arrival of the two teachers.

Adair hadn't met Miss Filby, and the other two officers hadn't met Miss Bennett, so a minute was spent on introductions.

When everyone was sitting down again, the DCI explained what was about to happen, and why he had asked for the two ladies to be present. Both were obviously astounded at the news about the Livermores, but quickly recovered.

"Let's hope we find the girls, Chief Inspector – and that they are unharmed," remarked Jackie Bennett.

"Amen to that. As I've just said to Miss Armstrong, if I've got this wrong my head is going to be on the block. I'll be a constable on point duty in Bognor Regis, or something. Ah, here are our reinforcements. Come in, Inspector."

Hatrick came into the room, with Borthwick following.

"I've parked my chaps in the waiting room, sir, and they've taken over the job of guarding your prisoner so your DS can join us here. I've got your map sheet."

He unrolled the plan, and spread it out on the table, using some books to hold down each corner.

"Excellent. Right, we're looking for Forty Acre Farm," said Adair.

"Ah, got it. Not a huge place, but a few outbuildings, by the look of it. Apparently only one way in from the road. But we need to get round the back very quickly.

Hatrick intervened. "If I might make a suggestion, sir." He pointed at the map. "We could post a couple of men in a car here, and with field glasses they could keep an eye on the back of the property – it'd only be two or three hundred yards away and there don't appear to be trees in the way. If anyone tried to escape over the fields they could nip down and intercept him."

"Excellent idea, Inspector. Are your cars equipped with binoculars?"

"Not as a rule, sir, but I brought a pair just in case."

"You'll go far. Just one addition to your plan – the officers in that car can take my prisoner with them – chances are they won't have to get out of the car, and if they do they can cuff her to the door. Oh, and arrange some sort of signal so you'll be able to tell them to abandon their position and return to the station.

"Right, basically this is what we'll do.

"Mr Hatrick, instruct your men about where to wait, and how to look after Mrs Livermore. You know the area, so you lead the rest of us. On arrival you take your other three men straight round to the back, and secure any exits there. Then come into the farmhouse one way or another – if Livermore is there you should really have the privilege of arresting him. Borthwick, Gemmill, you come to the front door with Mr Davison and me. If Livermore appears, and is arrested, one of you can sit him down somewhere, while we search.

"I don't think we can go into much more detail – we'll have to play it by ear.

Miss Filby, Miss Bennett, you'll come with Inspector Davison in my car, but you must remain in the car while we go into the house.

"Any questions? Good, let's go."

CHAPTER 12

Adair was introduced briefly to the five local officers, and then the four cars – two marked and two unmarked – swept down the drive and off towards the Kent Downs. A number of turns took the convoy onto a very minor road, and some ten minutes after starting out, Hatrick's car turned onto an unmade road. The two Yard cars followed. The second local car continued along the road. Since the farmhouse wasn't visible from this point, Hatrick's car stopped as agreed, to give the other car time to get into position. After waiting two minutes, his driver started off again, going as fast as possible over the bumpy track. The little farmhouse came into view, and while Hatrick's car drove around to the rear, the two Yard cars skidded to a halt at the front.

The two teachers, watching anxiously from their car, saw that one of the sergeants was carrying what looked like a log of wood – an object about eight inches in diameter and three feet long. It seemed to have handles of some sort, and as the officers arrived at the front door, the man swung it violently and there was a tremendous thud as it made contact. With a second blow, the door burst open, and the four detectives ran inside, and disappeared from view.

Nothing happened for six or seven minutes, and then Sergeant Gemmill appeared, picked up the wooden ram, and returned to the cars. He dumped his ram in the other car boot, and then came over to the teachers. He opened a rear door, grinning.

"Everything is fine, ladies. Mr Adair asks if you will come inside now. Please follow me."

Gemmill led the way past the broken door, and along a short passage to a kitchen. On the way, they passed a half-open door, and could hear the Chief Inspector talking.

In the kitchen, they found the two missing girls sitting at the table. Sergeant Borthwick was leaning against the door. Both children had clearly been crying, but were already looking more stoic. At the entrance of their teachers, they jumped up and after a second's hesitation (neither side being quite sure of the protocol), each was hugged by her teacher. Both women also had tears in their eyes.

"If you just stay in here a little longer, ladies, the DCI will come and talk to you shortly," said Borthwick. "But in the meantime, I'm to warn you that until the girls have made formal statements, you shouldn't discuss anything about what's happened – just talk about mundane things like lessons, or school meals, or something." He left the kitchen.

In the living room, which was furnished far more luxuriously than it would ever have been when the place was an active farm, Dr Livermore was sitting next to a burly constable – was handcuffed to him, in fact. Adair, Davison, and Hatrick were all standing, staring contemptuously at the dishevelled-looking man.

"I don't see any point in talking here, Livermore," said the DCI. "We'll get you to a police station now. Oh, and your wife is under arrest as well, by the way. But you won't be seeing her for some time – in fact probably not until you are both standing in the dock being committed for trial."

The Doctor visibly stiffened at that piece of information, but still said nothing.

In the hallway, Hatrick looked at the broken door. "This place is so far off the beaten track that I can't see we need fear burglars. If you're happy, sir, I'll get a chippy to come along in the morning and make it secure."

"Yes, that's fine, Inspector. My chaps will be searching the place tonight. Give the signal to your men on the hill, and then get Livermore to the station. I'll join you shortly. Don't mention a solicitor unless he does."

As the others left the farmhouse, and Davison went to talk to the sergeants, Adair walked the few yards to the kitchen.

He was very surprised indeed when both girls jumped up and hugged him. The teachers, far from reproving their pupils, smiled tolerantly.

"Thank you so much for rescuing us, sir," said each girl, almost in synchronism.

"It's my job," replied the DCI, much embarrassed. "Look. We're going to get you back to school now, and not bother you again today. I'm expecting both your fathers will be at Willowbank to meet you, and they'll have a lovely surprise as they don't yet know you've been found. Tomorrow, we'll have to talk to you, and you'll need to make statements. That won't be too difficult – and again a parent can be with you. Let's go now."

Outside, Adair directed the four females to get into his car. Inspector Hatrick's car had already left. "You stay with the sergeants, Inspector, and search the house. The place isn't very big, so it shouldn't take long. It would be good to find a typewriter. Go to the police station when you've done. I'll drive the ladies back to school, and then come to join you at the station."

On the way back, Jackie Bennett, sitting in the front beside Adair, turned towards him.

"I suppose this means no bridge this evening, Chief Inspector? I was so looking forward to that."

"I'm still looking forward to it. As you heard me say, I want to give Megan and Aaliyah an evening off. The Livermores will also wait until tomorrow. So I don't see why I shouldn't be available for a few games."

"I'd like to learn to play bridge," Aaliyah

called from the back seat. Must be worth it if you get to play with Scotland Yard detectives occasionally! I know some of the older girls play. Will you teach me sometime, please Miss?"

"I'll do that, Aaliyah. We'll have some lessons for anyone over a certain age who would like to learn. I would point out, though, that we all hope that we never have to have a police officer staying in the house again!"

"Just one thing," interrupted Adair, "isn't the playing of card games *haram* under Islamic law?"

"I believe it is, sir, yes," replied the girl. "But my family are Maronites – Christians – so it isn't a problem for me."

"I'm glad you drew our attention to that, Chief Inspector," said Miss Bennett. "It's something we'll need to bear in mind for the future, if not at the present time."

"It's all very well for you, Aaliyah," said Megan. "I know how to play bridge, but we don't have any facilities in Wollstonecraft."

"Well, we might be able to change that," said Miss Filby. "I can play, and we'll have to see if we can find a few others. Perhaps we'll get it added to the school curriculum. It would be nice, in a year or so, to have inter-house tournaments."

"Good idea," remarked Adair when he had managed to overtake a slow-moving horse and cart. "It's an activity where a thirteen-year-old can compete with an eighteen-year-old – or even with an adult."

A few minutes later, he pulled up outside the front door of the old school building.

"We'll all go along to Miss Armstrong's room first," he said.

They didn't meet anyone as they walked along the corridor. Tapping on the Head's door, the DCI ushered the four females inside, and followed them. Bedlam resulted. The Earl and Countess of Trimley, Mr Hammadani, and Miss Armstrong, all jumped to their feet, and ran towards the girls. Hammadani, a huge man, swung his daughter so high in the air that she almost collided with the crystal chandelier. Everyone was talking at once. After a full minute of chaos, things calmed down, and Miss Armstrong introduced the DCI to the parents. The two men immediately came over to him – Trimley shook his hand very fiercely, and didn't appear to want to release it. Hammadani, unable to get at Adair's right hand grabbed his left instead, and also flung his arm around the detective's shoulder. Both children joined in again too.

Lady Trimley, only slightly more restrained, put her hand on her husband's, and assisted him with the pumping.

Adair, once again embarrassed, was glad when he was eventually released.

"Congratulations, Chief Inspector," said the Headmistress. "It's not an exaggeration to describe you as the saviour of the school. Let's all sit down for a moment. I hope I haven't done anything wrong, but I felt I had to tell these parents what you were doing. So they know about the Livermores. What happens now?"

"Well, I suppose the first thing we should consider is seeing if we can find a lady doctor to examine these two youngsters."

The parents looked at each other, but Megan spoke before any of the adults could respond.

"We understand, Chief Inspector, but you needn't worry. Doctor Livermore never touched us – apart from the injection – and we were always fully clothed, so we'd really rather not be 'examined'.

"That seems to be all right, Chief Inspector," said Trimley. "If it's not necessary, let's skip it.

"Good. I'm going to the police station in a few minutes. Both the Livermores have been arrested on suspicion of kidnapping. I think we'll leave them in the cells to think about things overnight, and start interviews in the morning. They'll be charged sometime tomorrow, and appear before the magistrates later.

"Also tomorrow, I'll have to interview you two young ladies, and take formal statements. No need to go to the police station for that – we'll do it here. Your parents can be present during the interviews, of course. It does mean, I'm afraid girls, that you'll have to miss an hour or two of school.

"Please come to Miss Spencer's office at eight forty-five, Aaliyah. And Megan, please come at nine forty-five.

"I'd like to see the letter you received, m'lord, although again that can wait until tomorrow, assuming you are staying overnight. That letter will be a key exhibit at the trial. Also, Mr Hammadani, I have a letter I want to show you tomorrow – which will also be important for the trial. Incidentally, sir, I expect that you, like Lord Trimley, will have received a ransom demand in the post today – perhaps you might make enquiries to see if that is so."

Hammadani nodded. "I'll do that."

"We are all staying overnight, Chief Inspector," confirmed Lady Trimley. "Miss Armstrong has also kindly arranged for us to have dinner and breakfast with our respective daughters."

"Excellent, m'lady. I'll see you at dinner, then, Mr Hammadani, as I'm billeted in your daughter's house.

"One last thing. I know this will be difficult, girls, but I want you to try not to mention names to any of your friends at this stage. You can just say that you've been released, and the police are looking to prosecute someone. If you make it clear from the outset that you aren't allowed to say any more, I think everyone will cotton on very quickly. By lunch time tomorrow I'll be able to release you from that restriction."

"Don't worry, Chief Inspector," said Trimley. I guess Hammadani and I will be with our daughters all evening. We'll keep the wolves at bay!"

His fellow-father nodded, and Adair grinned.

"The same applies to you, ladies. Your task is the harder, Miss Filby, given that your Housemistress won't be appearing at dinner, but please do your best.

"Just one other thing, ma'am. Although Inspector Davison and I will be grateful for your hospitality again tonight, my two sergeants will be returning to London shortly. They'll come here in half an hour or so to search the Livermores' rooms, then they'll collect their bags and move out. Now, if you'll excuse me, I must go."

The DCI drove to the police station. In the foyer, he introduced himself to the Desk Sergeant, who snapped to attention.

"Your colleagues and Mr Hatrick are in the Super's office, sir – and the Chief Constable arrived a few minutes ago and he's in there too. Shall I show you up?"

"No thanks, Sergeant – just tell me where to go."

"Up the stairs, sir, second door on the left."

The DCI trotted up the stairs and tapped on the door marked '*Superintendent P Waller*'.

To a call of "come in", he opened the door and found his sergeants blocking the doorway. The Superintendent was seated at his desk, with Colonel Hardy sitting beside him. Inspectors Hatrick and Davison occupied the only other chairs, leaving Borthwick and Gemmill to stand in the remaining limited space.

Adair not having met the Super before, Hatrick performed a quick introduction, and stood to give his seat to the DCI.

"I think we can reduce the congestion a little," said Adair. "Borthwick, Gemmill, take your car and go back to the school. Do a thorough search of the Livermores' rooms – including their suitcases. Don't worry if you make a mess. If you find anything which might be connected to that letter, seize it. I assume you didn't find a typewriter at the farm, so see if you can find one in the house. I don't suppose we'll be that lucky. Wait in the office when you've finished. You two can go back to the Yard this evening, so pack your bags and move out of your quarters. But I expect to be back in Willowbank before you've finished the search so I'll see you before you leave."

The two men turned to go, the Chief Constable calling "Thank you, gentlemen" as they went out.

"Has either Livermore said anything?" asked Adair.

"Not a peep out of either of them, sir," replied Hatrick. "I booked both of them in, although we arranged it so they didn't see each other. He looked scared, and appeared to be about to speak, but didn't. She just looks furious."

"Very well. What I propose to do is this. We make no attempt to talk to them until mid-morning tomorrow. When their food is delivered, your officers should do so in silence, and refuse to answer if spoken to.

"Inspector Davison and I will interview the two girls in the morning, and get statements. Armed with those, we'll then come back here and see the Livermores. Him first, I fancy.

"Everyone happy?"

"Yes," said the Chief Constable. "You and your team have done very well, Adair, and nobody here is going to query your tactics now. I'll be informing the Commissioner that we are more than pleased."

"Thank you, sir. Come on, Davison."

***

"I hear you played contract bridge – whatever that is – yesterday evening, sir," said Davison on the way back to the school. "Given that Wollstonecraft doesn't seem to provide those facilities, and I don't play anyway, is it OK if I go down to the pub again?"

"Yes, of course. I should really join you, and not leave you on your own – but I don't get many chances for a decent game these days."

"That's all right sir. There were some interesting characters in the pub last night. I'll have some good conversations, I think."

The two officers found Miss Spencer rummaging through a filing cabinet again. Her face visibly brightened as the detectives entered.

"Oh, it's so good that you found the girls,"

she gushed. "I'd almost convinced myself that they'd been murdered. Can I get you a cup of tea or anything?"

Adair glanced at his colleague, who nodded.

"Yes please, Miss Spencer. We have an hour or so before dinner."

"May I tell Lucy that you're here, Chief Inspector? I know she wants a word."

"Yes, of course. We'll stay here."

The Secretary left via the interconnecting door, and a minute later Miss Armstrong came through. Both men had remained standing, and now the DCI indicated that the Head should take a seat. He sat opposite her at Miss Spencer's desk, and Davison sat on a chair in the corner of the room.

"I can't begin to tell you how grateful I am, Chief Inspector. There are two things, really.

"First, may I now inform the Governors and all the other parents? That'll be a lengthy task in itself, of course, with only two telephone lines.

"Second, there have been several calls from the Press. Will you be talking to some of the journalists? I'd really like to get them off my back."

"Well," replied the DCI, "by now I imagine every member of your staff, and every pupil, is aware of the fact that the girls are back safe.

"What I don't want publicised yet are the names of the perpetrators. I'd rather those are still kept quiet until they are actually charged.

"Perhaps you could make a statement on the

following lines to the Governors and the other parents:

"The girls are safe. Two people have been arrested on suspicion of child kidnapping and are in police custody. No further arrests are expected. A further announcement will be made sometime tomorrow."

"Thank you; that's ideal. Angela and I will start calling people."

"I'll speak to some press people, ma'am. Did you or your Secretary take any of the callers' numbers?"

Miss Spencer, coming in with a tray of tea, overheard the question and answered herself.

"Yes, I have half a dozen numbers, Chief Inspector. I'll bring them to you directly." She put down the tray, poured two cups of tea, and then left the room again.

The Head was just rising to her feet when the DCI spoke again.

"There is just one thing which is puzzling me. As I mentioned yesterday, in all the letters we found from Mr Hammadani to his daughter there was a short section of Arabic writing. There was also some in the letter which lured Aaliyah away.

"The question is, who composed that bit of writing? Unless either Dr or Mrs Livermore has colloquial Arabic, someone else helped them. Now, when Leila helped us with translation, she didn't pick up the point, and I'm also quite certain that I should have noticed if she had been evasive in any way.

"You said there was another Arabic speaker. I'd like to speak to her, please."

"Yes, there is Nadiyya – spelt n-a-d-i-y-y-a – Qadir, in the second year. She'll be back in her boarding house by now. She's in Somerville... Oh dear, I suppose that is significant. But I can't believe she'd do anything to harm Aaliyah."

"Oh, if she did anything I'm sure there was no malice aforethought, ma'am."

As the Secretary came back with the telephone numbers, Adair addressed her directly.

"Please go over to Somerville, Miss Spencer, and bring Nadiyya here at once."

Without even looking at the Headmistress, the Secretary put her paper down on the desk, and went out.

"Perhaps you might stay, ma'am – *in loco parentis*, as it were."

"Yes. Yes, I suppose I should."

"I'll make a couple of these calls while we wait."

Adair looked at the names and numbers on the list, and then picked up the telephone. In two minutes he was speaking to a reporter. After identifying himself, he dictated his short statement.

"No, I'm not answering any further questions today. But if you come to the town police station tomorrow at one p.m., you may learn more."

The DCI made two further calls, each time declining to take questions, and again offering the appointment the next day. After the third call, he replaced the receiver.

"That's the local paper sorted, plus Reuters and the Press Association, who will pass it around. The reporters will be off your back now, hopefully."

Inspector Davison, sitting sipping his tea, now spoke.

"Do you think the Livermores will stay silent tomorrow, sir?"

"No. I expect the Doctor to start by admitting everything. Not much else he can do, really, as he was caught *in flagrante delicto*, that's as the lawyers use the term, without implying the common meaning. But then I expect him to accuse his wife of plotting the whole thing and forcing him to participate.

"She may stick to stout denial, and say she had no knowledge of the plan, and back that up by saying that she threw him out because he was an unstable and unreasonable man.

"But if she hears that he's saying that she's the driving force, it may be that she'll decide to say that it was all his idea. Time will tell.

"You see, ma'am, we policemen rather like to see people employing what's called the 'cut-throat defence'. It usually means that we don't have to prove quite so many things – and it frequently means that the jury convicts both defendants."

"But why did she do this?"

"I really have no idea. But I hope to find out tomorrow."

There was silence in the room for a moment, and then the Secretary arrived, escorting a frightened-looking child of about twelve.

"Thank you Miss Spencer. Just hang on for a minute, if you please. Now, young lady, do sit down. There is absolutely nothing for you to worry about, and we won't keep you for many minutes. My name is Adair, and this is Mr Davison. We're policemen, as I'm sure you know. I just need to ask you a couple of questions. You know how important it is to tell the truth, of course – especially in a situation like this where a horrible crime has occurred."

The girl spoke in perfect English, but with a delightful accent. "Yes, of course, sir – but I didn't have anything to do with this."

"No, no, I'm sure you didn't. But you still may be able to help.

"At some time – I don't know whether it was quite recently or a few weeks ago, did someone ask you to write out one or two Arabic phrases? I don't suppose such a thing would happen very often."

The girl stared at him in surprise, and then her face cleared suddenly.

"Why yes," she exclaimed. "It was about a week ago. I'd been a bit naughty, and Mrs Livermore gave me some lines as punishment. She said something about how it must take longer to write something in Arabic than it would in

English, so she gave me some English sentences and told me to write them in Arabic for her."

"That's good, Nadiyya. Can you remember the English version of anything she gave you to translate?

"A bit, sir. There was something about school tests, and one line said something like 'I'm proud of you'. There was a line about holidays, too."

"Thank you, Nadiyya. Would I be right in thinking that although you and Aaliyah have a common language, you don't really know her?"

That's right, sir. I know her by sight, but we're in different years and different houses. I've never even spoken to her."

"No," said Adair *sotto voce*. "She banked on that. Guessed the sense of the snippets and got a new one ready."

"Sir?"

"No, sorry, Nadiyya; I was talking to myself. Now, we just need you to write a short statement about what you've just told us, and then you can get back to your house for the evening meal. Inspector – just get the essentials down. Four or five sentences should suffice."

A few minutes later the statement was written and signed. Adair, who had been conversing quietly with Miss Armstrong, turned back to the girl.

"This must seem very baffling to you, young lady. But in a day or so you'll probably learn why what you have told us is important."

Nadiyya looked at him thoughtfully. "Perhaps I could guess, sir. Was Aaliyah tempted to go with someone because a letter written with some Arabic in it made her think it was genuine?"

Not for the first time since arriving at the school, the DCI was surprised at the acuity demonstrated by such a young child.

"Something of that sort, perhaps. Please don't talk to anyone about this today – we need to keep it secret for now."

"I understand, sir. But will everyone know that I did something to help get the two girls kidnapped?"

"It will probably come out in the trial – it's just possible you may even be called to give evidence, although I think that's very unlikely. But anybody hearing the facts will know that there is absolutely no blame attached to you. Please don't even think about it. Off you go now – Miss Spencer will see you back to your house.

"Presumably you'll be on the telephone most of the evening, ma'am?"

"Alas, yes. I'll get Angela to use the other telephone line in Bill's office. In fact I think I'll have to look into sending telegrams – I've never done this, but perhaps it's possible to dictate one message, and have that sent to lots of different addresses.

"Enjoy your bridge after dinner, Chief Inspector."

Seeing Adair's surprised expression, the

Head smiled. "Oh, my grapevine usually works. I have to confess it let me down over Harvey, and over the Livermores, but we can't get it right all the time.

"Of course, you'll be able to play again if you stay overnight when you come to address the school."

Adair gave a resigned laugh. "You win, ma'am."

Both officers stood as she left the room.

"She'll have her work cut out to restore the good name of the school," remarked Davison. "And the bigamy matter coming on top of the kidnapping won't help."

"Very true. But I imagine the parents we've seen will help to spread the word that everything is OK now – and even Colonel Hardy will do his bit.

"You'll have gathered what the Headmistress asked me while you were helping Nadiyya with her statement. She wants me to come and give a talk to the school about Scotland Yard. I knew that they invite all sorts of civil servants, business people, judges, and so on – but apparently they've never had a detective before! I was under pressure to accept the invitation, but hadn't actually said 'yes'. Then she offers an evening of bridge, correctly believing that'll tip the scale."

He was still shaking his head when the two sergeants returned.

"Sorry, sir, nothing relevant to report. No

typewriter – probably in a river by now."

"Never mind. We've found the child who inadvertently helped Mrs L to write the Arabic in the false letter. That's as good as the typewriter – perhaps better.

"Right, you two get back to London. Make your statements tomorrow. Good evening."

***

Adair returned to Lovelace just as everyone was ready to go into dinner. Miss Fleming quickly whispered that Aaliyah and her Father had both requested that he sit with them, and he found that he was placed at one end of table 4, with Mr Hammadani at the other.

After grace, the children all began to chatter. The atmosphere – although not especially sombre during his previous meals in the dining hall – was now very cheerful. Hammadani – who in impeccable English told the children that he had been educated at Winchester – was a sparkling conversationalist. He and Adair between them kept the subjects well away from Aaliyah's ordeal, and the meal passed happily. The DCI admitted to the girls nearest to him that he was enjoying his stay in the school – except for having to serve food equitably to eight or nine people while still leaving sufficient for himself!

After the meal, Alice approached the DCI and told him that the bridge tonight would be in Miss Bennett's room, and led him to the room he had briefly visited before. Here, two tables had been squeezed in, and several girls were already waiting. Adair was introduced to Olivia, Jennifer, and Tamsin – who looked to be no older than Aaliyah, but she informed him that she was actually sixteen.

"Miss Fleming apologises, Chief Inspector," said the House Tutor, "but she remembered that she's on 'rounds' duty this evening, and as she barred Alice from playing last night, feels it's only fair to disqualify herself tonight. By the way, I know you were told that we drop formality in these sessions – I'm Jackie and I hope you don't mind everyone calling you David.

"Now, I'm told that Leah was promised that she could partner you for the first rubber tonight, so the rest of us will cut.

The cutting allocated Alice and Olivia to oppose Adair and Leah. At the other table, Miss Bennett and Tamsin faced Jennifer and Francesca. Adair and his partner triumphed by two games to none. Progress was at much the same pace at the second table, where the House Tutor and Tamsin also won 2-nil.

Another round of cutting pitted the DCI and Tamsin against Miss Bennett and Alice. This time things were a little more even, but the partnership of the oldest and youngest players eventually won by two games to one.

Adair had genuinely enjoyed the evening, and thanked everyone warmly. When the others had gone, he spoke again.

"I do hope the other houses pick up on the discussion in the car, Jackie. I feel that bridge is beneficial in many ways. Improving card memory is a useful skill which I believe is transferable to other activities. There's some mathematics. There is the need to be able to work together with a partner. There is the development of the sometimes-derided mindset of wanting to win."

"Oh, I so agree," exclaimed the teacher. "Laura and I will certainly work on the idea."

"I can approach your Head with an endorsement if that would help – just let me know. I've been pressured into coming to address the school, so if you haven't succeeded in convincing the powers-that-be by then, I'll have to proselytise!

"My six-year-old daughter can't hold a hand of cards properly yet – but my wife and I intend to teach her the game in the next couple of years. Anyway, I wish you goodnight – I'll see you at breakfast."

CHAPTER 13

The next morning, Adair found himself allocated to the table from which he had left early the day before, to the delight of the girls there. He answered several questions about previous cases in which he'd been involved and was then asked about female police officers.

"The Metropolitan Police appointed its first female officers soon after the war. I'm afraid they came in for a lot of ridicule – and opposition from a variety of people. Initially, they were very restricted. They weren't even attested – that means they didn't have a constable's power of arrest – until 1923. Although in Lincolnshire a woman was appointed as a fully attested constable much earlier – in 1915, I think. We still don't have women in the CID at Scotland Yard. I don't know if there are any outside London.

"Before anyone asks for my opinion, I'll give it to you. I think there is certainly a case for having female detectives. You have to understand that detectives must serve in the uniformed branch first. So, as the numbers of females there rise, there will come a time when some are eligible to volunteer to transfer into the CID. I'm sure that there will be female detectives quite soon."

After a pause for eating, a girl who had so far remained silent, spoke.

"We heard you have a wonderful memory, sir – putting names to all the faces around the table after hearing them only once. All the other tables have been impressed, and of course you've been doing it here this morning. I think we'd all like to have that sort of memory, so we could sail through exams and so on. Is there a secret?"

"I don't think so, Bernice. As some of you know, I play bridge, and it is essential in that game to have a good memory – not just for what cards have already been played, but for what people bid during the auction earlier. I think it's more a question of practice than of learning some secret.

"But, you see, in that sort of situation I don't retain much of what I take in. By now, for example, I probably couldn't name all the girls I sat with at lunch on Tuesday, although as you say I could do so easily at the time. Nor could I tell you much about the bridge I played last night, although when I went to bed I could have described every hand. So if I was revising for an examination which was to be held next Monday, if I used that part of my brain to revise, what I took in today would mostly be gone by then.

"I'm no brain expert, but I think there are two parts to our memories – short-term and long-term. I only have a modest long-term one!"

"How much of your deduction comes from painstaking routine enquiries, sir, and how much from brilliant flashes of inspiration?" asked another girl.

Adair laughed.

"Practically none from the latter, in my experience, Harriet. Almost all via routine work. I have never met any detective who has the sort of attributes which crime authors give their protagonists. Sherlock Holmes, Hercule Poirot, and the others simply don't exist in real life.

"I can't go into detail about this particular case, but I will let you into a secret. The breakthrough came as a result of a chance remark made by one of your junior colleagues over dinner. It set me thinking, and made me realise that I had omitted to do something vital. So no flash of brilliance on my part – rather the reverse."

After breakfast, the DCI walked over to the old house, where he found Inspector Davison talking to the Headmistress and the Secretary in the latter's office.

"Did you sleep well after your victories at the bridge table?" Chief Inspector," queried Miss Armstrong.

"Your grapevine is working overtime, ma'am; yes very well, thank you.

"The Inspector here was just telling us that he also spent the evening playing cards – in his case cribbage at the Lion and Lamb. A game which certainly predates bridge, and probably even whist."

"I'm sure you're right, ma'am," smiled Adair. "However, with respect to the Inspector and his perfectly honourable predilection, I don't think crib has quite the same *cachet* as bridge.

"I should tell you, though, that the subject came up as I was bringing the girls back yesterday – Megan knows the game, and was bemoaning the fact that there is no facility for playing with the staff in her house, as there is in Lovelace – Miss Filby was supportive. And Aaliyah was begging Miss Bennett to teach her."

"Oh, you don't need to tell me that Laura Filby is supportive. I saw Jackie this morning – it's from her that I heard about your triumphs – and she also expounded what she said were your views on the benefits of the game. I'm not unsympathetic! Anyway I must get along. Angela, come through now, please."

"I hope you weren't gambling in the pub, Davison," said Adair with a smile.

"We weren't, actually, sir. But the night before, one of the locals said 'you must be the policemen come to find these missing children', and we couldn't really deny it. So it's possible that last night when the cards came out the locals showed a bit of discretion."

The DCI laughed. "Yes, and I bet the Landlord put some pressure on too. Last thing he wants is you talking to the licensing justices!"

"We seem to be doing OK on this now, sir – I can't see that Livermore has a defence. His wife might be a bit more tricky – a pity the lads couldn't find the typewriter."

"True. But we have the evidence of Nadiyya, circumstantial though it is. And it's just possible that Mrs L was stupid enough to leave her prints on the letter."

Adair was just about to expand on this when a knock on the door presaged the arrival of Mr Hammadani and his daughter.

When everyone was seated, Hammadani spoke.

"Before we start, Chief Inspector, I telephoned my London house after dinner last night. You were quite correct. There is a letter. I instructed a member of my staff to put on thin gloves and then open it very carefully. Just like Trimley's, I gather – a demand for fifty thousand pounds. I didn't bother to find you last night – I assume the only interest now is fingerprints, and there didn't seem much urgency for that. Letter and envelope are being brought down here this morning – you'll have it by lunchtime."

"Thank you, sir. I don't hold out much hope of fingerprints, but one never knows."

"Aaliyah has told me about the letter she received, gentlemen," continued Hammadani. "Presumably it's the one you said last night that you wanted to show me?"

"That's right, sir. Take a look now – I'm

afraid it's a bit messy with fingerprint dust."

He pushed the letter across the table.

"But how did you find it, sir?" asked the girl. "I hid it carefully."

"You did, yes. But there had to be something that persuaded you to leave the school and go with someone. Either some authority figure in the school persuaded you orally, or you received a note or a letter – apparently from someone you trusted but actually initiated by such a person. So I searched your study.

"The letter says, of course, that you mustn't tell anyone what you are going to do. But it doesn't tell you to destroy the letter – that might have aroused your suspicions. We know that Mrs Livermore had previously found a number of letters from your father, and that you left them more-or-less openly in your study. I think that she probably slipped back in there after you'd been abducted, and when she couldn't find the fake one assumed – wrongly – that you were carrying it with you."

"This letter is certainly a good forgery, Chief Inspector. I know that it must seem rather odd that I send typed letters to my beloved daughter, but for many years I've found it far easier to dictate than to write with a pen. And, as you've no doubt observed, I have different secretaries using different typewriters. They are Arabic speakers, naturally, and so even my little notes are written in different hands. It was all too easy for these

Livermore people.

"Even this last one: 'I'm so proud of you', is exactly what I might – indeed should – have written. However, it doesn't appear to have been written by someone who has Arabic as their first language, Chief Inspector. Copied from somewhere else, I think."

"Quite correct, sir. We know how Mrs Livermore obtained that, and the person concerned is entirely innocent of any wrongdoing.

"Now, young lady, I don't want to cause you any upset, but I need you to go over what happened on Monday. Start with when you received the letter. Inspector Davison here has pretty good shorthand skills, so he'll be making a note of what you say."

"Well, I went back to the house in the morning break, to see if there were any letters. The postman comes about ten o'clock, you see. I do that sometimes, although other days I wait until we all go back for lunch.

"So I saw the letter in my pigeon-hole, and realised at once that it was from Daddy. I took it back to my study to read. By then I only had about ten minutes before I had to be back in school, you see. Anyway, I read it quickly – I never had any doubt that it was genuine. I took in what it said, and thought that if I mustn't tell anyone I'd better not leave it lying around, so I tucked it inside my Latin primer. I went back to school, and was lucky enough to see Megan all by herself just coming out of the lavatory. So I told her what the letter said – that her father and mine would be taking the two of us out for a treat that very evening. She didn't query anything either – just looked very pleased. As you know, the letter told us to leave by separate doors a few minutes apart, and go round to the back of the swimming pool. So I did that."

She paused, and looked upset.

"I was really stupid, I know."

"No, Aaliyah – this was a very well-planned and well-executed scheme. I think any other girl of your age would have been deceived. Go on, please."

"Yes, well this is the nasty bit. I left the building, and went round the corner as instructed. Before I knew what was happening, I was grabbed by someone – at that stage I didn't see who it was – and I felt a smelly cloth held over my face. I must have passed out almost at once. At some point he gave me an injection, because the next day when I mentioned a sore place on my leg he told me he'd given both of us something to keep us unconscious for longer.

"Anyway, when I woke up, I was lying on a big bed. Megan was beside me, still unconscious. I had no idea where we were, but there were bars on the windows, as you saw sir, when you came to let us out.

"After a bit Megan woke up. We both had headaches, but we tried to get out, and found that the door was locked, of course. We had a bathroom attached to the bedroom, and the windows were also barred in there. We talked for ages. I don't mind admitting that we were very scared, but it was far better than it would have been if each of us had been alone.

"Then Dr Livermore came in, and that was when we first knew what this was all about. I knew him by sight, but I'd never spoken to him before. He was quite open about kidnapping us, saying that our parents were going to pay a lot of money into a fund that was going to provide a very nice pension for him and his wife for the rest of their lives.

"He told us that we'd have to stay where we were for two or three days, and that nothing would happen to us if our parents co-operated. But he said that he'd beat us if we made any attempt to escape.

"We didn't see much of him after that. He brought food, which wasn't too bad, really. The next day he brought some breakfast, and then we heard his car leaving. He was away for several hours, and when he came back he said that our parents now knew what the price for our release would be. We cried a bit, then, because we thought that he couldn't ever let anyone see us after the ransom was paid, and he'd just kill us."

He must have realised what we thought, because he made an attempt to reassure us. Apparently he and his wife would be on the way to some foreign country where they could never be handed back, and information would be left behind so that we would only be found when it was too late to stop them leaving the country. I suppose we did sort of believe him – we wanted to.

"Then yesterday after what passed for lunch we heard cars arriving, and there was a great big bang, and lots of voices. Next thing we knew was you unlocking the door, and telling us to go and wait in the kitchen with your Sergeant, and Miss Bennett and Miss Filby came in to look after us. It was kind of you to bring them, sir."

Hammadani stirred. This was a dreadful experience for the two girls, Chief Inspector. The only positive aspect is that you found them very quickly and they haven't been physically harmed. What will happen to these criminals?"

"Well, sir, the first step is to get a jury to convict them. Hopefully straightforward in Dr Livermore's case, but we still have work to do on the woman's. Kidnapping is a very serious offence, of course, but what Aaliyah has told us means I'll be adding a further charge. Administering chloroform or other stupefying drug in the course of committing another felony is itself an offence – punishable by penal servitude for life."

"Good. I appreciate that's the best you can offer. But summary execution would be more to my taste."

Adair diplomatically said nothing, and Davison started talking to Aaliyah about wording for her statement.

Half an hour later, the statement was

written, and signed.

"That's it, young lady – back to school for you, unless your father has made other arrangements. All this was a very unpleasant experience, of course, and it would be foolish of me to suggest you can just forget it. But you mustn't brood over it. I may see you again, incidentally, as your Head has persuaded me to come and address the school on life at Scotland Yard!"

The girl grinned. Perhaps I'll have learned how to play bridge by then sir. And thank you again. She turned and went out.

Hammadani shook hands with both detectives, thanked them again, and followed his daughter.

Adair's scheduling estimate was working well, because only two minutes after the Hammadanis left, the Innes-Fieldings arrived.

When all five people were seated, Lord Trimley produced the ransom letter he had received.

"I suppose this is of little use now, unless you have found the typewriter, or you can find somebody's fingerprints on it," he remarked.

"That's right, m'lord. We haven't found the typewriter, but we'll certainly check the letter for prints. We now know that Mr Hammadani received a similar demand, and his letter is being sent down here this morning for us to check that too.

"Now, Megan, we've heard from Aaliyah – how she received the letter purporting to come from her father, and how she passed the information to you. Please tell us, in your own words, what happened after school on Monday."

"There's not much to tell, really. Aaliyah said that we must keep this completely quiet, as other girls would be jealous if we were allowed out for a treat when we'd both used up our exeats for the half-term. I was to go out of the door by the science block, and after the last lesson I just slipped out without anyone noticing. I walked round to the pool as instructed. It was dark, of course. I was suddenly grabbed by someone, and this horrible damp cloth with a funny smell was pressed over my nose and mouth. I tried to scream but couldn't. Then I must have passed out.

"When I woke up, I was in a bedroom somewhere, I had no idea where. Aaliyah was there with me – she woke before me I think. I had an awful headache. We talked, and quickly realised we'd been kidnapped. We didn't know who did it – I hadn't seen who attacked me, and nor had Aaliyah. We tried the door, but it was locked – and it was a really solid door. There were bars in the window. There was another door leading to a bathroom, and I went in there to be sick. There were bars on the window in the bathroom too.

"When it got light the next morning we could see from the window that we were in some place right out in the countryside – there were no other houses in sight.

"Anyway, after a while the first evening, we heard someone coming up the stairs, and then Dr Livermore came in. For a second I thought he'd come to rescue us, but of course he hadn't – he was the kidnapper.

"He told us we'd be quite safe, if our parents paid a lot of money. He spoke of putting it in a Swiss bank, and then he and his wife would leave this country and be able to retire somewhere else.

"Aaliyah said something had made her leg sore, and he said that after he'd given us something to make us unconscious, he'd given each of us an injection to keep us asleep longer until he could get us to his prison place. He put us in his car boot, he said."

Do you remember what he told you he used to make you unconscious to start with?" asked the DCI.

"Oh yes, sir, he said chloroform. I've read about that. They still use it sometimes in operations and things, don't they? I don't think he told us what injection he gave us.

"Well, there isn't much more. He brought us food from time to time. It was very boring, actually. We had no books, or a radio, or anything. The second day he was away for ages, and when he came back he said he'd told our parents what they had to do to get us back safe.

"He wasn't nasty or unkind, or anything, although he did threaten to thrash us if we tried to escape. I thought he was quite nervous, actually – not as scared as we were, but not like the cheerful-looking Doctor we see around the school – and after he married a Housemistress and moved in we saw him more often, of course. In my first year I only spoke to him twice, when I was ill. He seemed quite nice, but I've never spoken to him since.

"Then yesterday we suddenly heard lots of people arriving, and voices, and then you came and unlocked the door. And that's it."

"That's excellent, Megan. Just a couple of questions, and then we'll get something written down that you can sign.

"You said he mentioned that he and his wife would be able to retire on the money your parents would be providing. Did he say anything else about her?"

"No, I don't think so, sir."

"There was a telephone in the house where you were held captive. Did you hear him talking on it?"

Megan shook her head. "If he did use it I didn't hear. But we didn't hear anything from downstairs anyway, apart from the bang when you broke in, and all the shouting. We never heard him moving about, or clattering pans in the kitchen, or anything. The walls are quite thick, I expect."

"All right, you've done well. Inspector Davison will help you with your statement now."

Adair turned to Lord and Lady Trimley, who had been sitting silently while their daughter recounted her story.

"In a few minutes, we'll be going to interview the Livermores. I don't know what – if anything – they'll say. But I'll charge them this morning anyway. It's possible one or both will plead guilty, but I'm not betting on that. If they don't, then I'm afraid Lady Megan will be a key prosecution witness at the Assizes in a few months' time. And perhaps before then in the preliminary proceedings in the Magistrates' Court.

"Yes, of course. I'm a magistrate myself – our little Bench doesn't see many committals."

So what do you think, Chief Inspector?" asked Lady Trimley. "Is it a cast-iron case?"

"Against him, yes, m'lady. Against her, I'm not so confident. But rest assured we'll work very hard to find whatever evidence we need to secure a conviction."

"Well, you and your team have done brilliantly so far," remarked the peer. "I know a lot of the top people, as you can imagine, and I'll certainly be mentioning your name in a very favourable manner."

"Very kind of you, m'lord, but I'm only doing my job."

Trimley snorted. "Doing it very well, then. Another thing. Megan tells us you discussed playing bridge, and that you'll support Miss Filby in getting the game introduced in those houses which don't have it. Amanda and I love bridge, and a year or so ago we taught Megan the basics of the game."

"Yes, and in fact both Miss Filby and I spoke independently to Miss Armstrong on the subject this morning. But no doubt your opinion will weigh more heavily than mine!"

Adair ended the meeting as he had with Aaliyah, telling Megan that she must treat the episode as an unpleasant experience, but not to dwell on it.

CHAPTER 14

On arrival at the police station, the detectives were greeted by the Desk Sergeant.

"Your woman has asked for a solicitor, sir, and the Super has okayed the request. Mr Wentworth is in with her now. The man still hasn't said anything, but I reckon he's near to wetting himself.

"All right – I wanted to see him first anyway. Have him brought out, please.

"Very good, sir. Mr Wentworth is seeing his client in Interview Room 1, and Room 2 is next door with a thin wall. Mr Hatrick has just gone out, but he anticipated the problem, and he suggests you use his office for the interviews. It's the one next to the Super's, where you went yesterday."

"Excellent; we'll go up. Thank you, Sergeant."

The two Yard officers trotted up the stairs, passed the Superintendent's door and found, as promised, that the next one read *'Inspector J Hatrick'*. They went inside; Adair sat in the Inspector's chair; Davison placed a chair beside him, and took out his pocket book in readiness. They didn't have long to wait.

There was a knock at the door, and Dr Livermore was shepherded into the room.

"Thank you Constable," said the DCI. "You can take off the bracelets. No need to hang around either – he isn't going to escape the two of us."

The detectives had only seen Livermore for a couple of minutes the day before, and now took a closer look at him. They saw a bespectacled man in his early forties, in need of a shave. His suit looked to be of good quality, but had of course been slept in. As the Sergeant had said, it was clear that the man was in a blue funk, and was shaking visibly.

"All right, Doctor," said Adair at last. "The caution you were given yesterday still applies. So let's get down to brass tacks. You kidnapped two children, and were caught red-handed. Tell us about it."

"It was Eleanor," replied Livermore, almost in tears. "She had the idea that we could make a huge amount of money, and then we'd go and live abroad somewhere."

"Somewhere that didn't have an extradition treaty with this country, I assume?"

"That's right. Our passports and visas are all arranged. And passage booked on a non-British ship. Once we'd cleared British waters, the idea was to get the captain to radio the coastguard or someone, and so tell the police how to find the girls."

"How very considerate of you. Go back a stage. How were the girls selected?"

"Initially Eleanor said we should choose the girl with the richest parent. That wasn't so easy, as almost all of them are pretty well off. But anyway, she later decided that if we could take two, that would be better – we might get two ransoms, or if one parent baulked at paying at least we'd have a chance with the other. In fact, Eleanor was absolutely certain that the parents of the two she picked out would choose to pay up without involving the police – and she pointed out that neither set of parents would really notice the loss of the money we would demand."

"How were the girls to be persuaded to leave the school?"

"Eleanor had this idea. When carrying out an inspection in Lovelace one day, she saw several letters from the father of the middle-eastern girl. Seeing them gave her an idea, and she brought one back to our house. Because it was mainly typed, it would be so easy to copy, she said. We could produce another, telling the girl what to do."

"Did you see the genuine letter?"

"Oh yes. It had this bit of Arabic writing in it."

"Who produced the fake letter?"

"She did. We had a typewriter. Have you seen the letter yourselves?"

"Oh yes, Doctor. What happened to the typewriter?"

"I drove up to London to post the letter – it had to carry a London postmark, obviously – and I dropped the typewriter into the Thames."

"You mentioned the piece of Arabic writing in the original letter. How was that dealt with in the forgery?"

"There's a girl in our house who speaks Arabic. Eleanor used some pretext to get her to write the phrase she wanted to use – 'I'm so proud of you'. Then she practised writing those letters out – did that over several days, actually, until she was satisfied her lettering was near enough to the examples in the other letters she'd seen. She typed the letter, added the Arabic bit, and forged the father's signature which she had also been practising. We burned all the practice sheets."

"Did you know either of these girls yourself?"

"No. I saw Lady Megan a couple of years ago, when she was ill – that was before I married Eleanor, but I've not spoken to her – I don't think I've even seen her – since then. I know the girls in our house, of course, but neither of these girls is in Wollstonecraft. Unless they're ill, I don't meet any of the others because I spend most of my day away from the school."

"All right; according to your story your wife instigated this crime, and was the chief organiser. Without commitment, we'll accept that for the moment. We'll also gloss over the reason for your tamely agreeing to go along with the scheme.

"Let's look now at your own undeniable actions. You knew that the girls – if they followed instructions – would appear from different directions behind the swimming pool. What did you do?"

"I must emphasise that I'm ashamed of what I did, Chief Inspector. But I had a bottle of chloroform and a lint pad. It was dark, and I stood where what light there was showed the girls and not me. I took hold of the first girl, and pressed the chloroform-laden pad over her face. She lost consciousness very quickly. Then I moved further along to await the second. She came as expected, and I dealt with her too. I suppose it took two minutes from start to finish."

"But you weren't satisfied with the chloroform, were you?"

"Well, no. I had to put both the girls in the boot of my car – just in case anyone saw them while I was driving along and became suspicious. The dose of chloroform almost certainly wouldn't have lasted until I reached my house, so I gave each of them an injection of morphine. That way I could ensure that they remained unconscious until I could get them safely locked up. I picked each of them up, and placed them in the boot. When I reached my house, I carried them upstairs one at a time and shut them in the bedroom."

"Yes – and you had previously done some alterations there, hadn't you – installing bars on the windows, and strengthening the bedroom door? Or are you saying your wife did all that?"

Livermore didn't reply.

"What about this business of leaving your wife?"

"That was also her idea. It meant that nobody would wonder why my car wasn't parked outside Wollstonecraft. So after dusk that evening, I drove in through the rear entrance gates, and parked behind the swimming pool. It was extremely unlikely that anyone would see me on the back drive, and wouldn't be able to identify the car in the dark anyway. Certainly nobody would be around the swimming pool at that time. When I'd got the girls, I drove out via the rear entrance again."

"You have a telephone in your farmhouse – it must have cost you a fortune to have it connected. Have you spoken to your wife since abducting the girls?"

"No. The boarding houses don't have telephones, only the main school building. I couldn't call her, and it was too risky for her to call me from there. I had the telephone installed here before I was married – and it certainly was expensive – because as a doctor I needed to be on call."

"All right. Are you prepared to make a statement?"

"I suppose so, I can hardly deny my part in this, although what I've told you about my wife is completely true."

Half an hour later, Livermore's agreed statement was written down and signed.

"That's it then," said Adair with a sigh.

"Keith Livermore, I charge you with kidnapping Lady Megan Innes-Fielding and Aaliyah Hammadani, on Monday last. I also charge you with administering a stupefying drug to the same persons, with the intent to assist in the commission of an indictable offence.

"The first matter is a Common Law offence; the second is contrary to Section 22 of the Offences Against the Person Act, 1861. Both carry a maximum penalty of penal servitude for life. But even if you are ever released, you'll never practise medicine again – you'll be 'struck off' by the General Medical Council very soon.

"You'll appear before the magistrates' court in the morning. If you want a solicitor, tell the Custody Sergeant downstairs.

"Take him downstairs, Inspector, get them to put him back in his cell, and see if you can find out how long before we can see the wife."

The Inspector was back within five minutes, accompanied by a young man, evidently the Solicitor, although he didn't look old enough to be qualified. They found the DCI standing by the window, apparently looking blankly at the sky.

"This is Mr Wentworth, sir. They'll bring Mrs Livermore up in a few minutes."

Adair extended his hand. "Anything you want to say before your client arrives?"

"No, thank you, Chief Inspector. She's made her position pretty clear to me."

"Good. Well, we'll have to see what she tells us."

"What's the situation with her husband?" asked the young lawyer.

"We'll hear from her first, I think, but I can tell you that he needs a solicitor – and he'll soon need counsel."

Wentworth hesitated. "I won't be able to represent him, Chief Inspector."

"I'm hardly surprised about that, Mr Wentworth. I have a wager as to whether Mrs Livermore will stick to 'stout denial of any knowledge', or if she'll employ the 'cut-throat defence'. Either way, you'd be disqualified from representing him."

The Solicitor looked discomfited for a moment, but quickly recovered, and a boyish grin spread over his face. "Ah well, you'll soon see."

Seconds later, Mrs Livermore was brought into the room.

"Do sit down," instructed the DCI. "I remind you that you have been cautioned, and that still applies.

"Now, Mr Wentworth, does your client want to make a statement at this stage, or would you prefer me to ask questions?"

"Please ask your questions, Chief Inspector – but I may advise her not to answer some of them."

"Fair enough. Your husband is in custody,

madam. He admits the drugging and kidnap of the two girls from your school. Indeed, since he was caught with the girls locked up in his house he could hardly do otherwise. What do you say about that?"

Mrs Livermore spoke for the first time.

"My husband and I separated. I have no idea why he should do such a thing unless it was to avenge himself on me for throwing him out."

"In what way would kidnapping innocent children be avenging himself on you?"

"Because it would probably ruin the school, and if the school closed then I should no longer have a job."

"I see. A somewhat obscure and complicated way of seeking revenge. But whatever.

"So your position is that you had no prior knowledge of his actions?"

"Correct."

"Nor did you have any inkling, when the girls were found to be missing, that he might have been involved?"

"Correct again."

"We now know that Aaliyah was lured into leaving school on Monday afternoon – and was also persuaded to invite Megan to join her – after receiving a letter purporting to come from her father."

"That is news to me. I suppose she told you this?"

"Actually no, Mrs Livermore. We found the

letter before we found the girls. It makes for very interesting reading. There are fingerprints on it, other than Aaliyah's."

The woman made no reply, but both Adair and Davison, experienced in reading people's faces, thought she looked a little surprised.

"You didn't realise we'd actually got hold of it, did you?"

"I don't know what you mean."

"Oh, I think you do. I believe you went back into Aaliyah's study, thinking she'd have left it with the others from her father. But she hadn't, so you wrongly assumed she'd taken it with her."

"I think you need to explain what this letter is all about," said Wentworth. "I don't know what you are talking about, and despite what you are implying, it's clear that my client doesn't either."

"I'll explain it to you by all means, Mr Wentworth. A letter, identical in format to others received by Aaliyah from her father, and apparently also from him, was sent to the girl. In it, she was told that her father, together with Megan Innes-Fielding's father, would take both girls out that evening for an unexpected treat. The letter gave instructions on what to tell Lady Megan, and on where to go. All very clandestine."

"I see," said the Solicitor. "But my client knows nothing of this letter."

"So she says. Well, let's examine the facts. The series of letters was kept in Aaliyah's study. Dr Livermore, if he goes into a boarding house other than the one he lives in, it would only be to see a sick child. He would go to the sick bay. No way would he ever enter a single study. But in fact Dr Livermore has never been to treat Aaliyah anyway – and she has never ever spoken to him. I think we can conclude that he didn't take one of the originals to copy."

"Circumstantial only, Chief Inspector," retorted the Solicitor.

"True. But then we look at the alternative. You, Mrs Livermore, go into all the boarding houses quite frequently – often by yourself. One of your official duties is to do just that – to inspect. So I deduce that you, unlike your husband, had ample opportunity."

"Ridiculous," snorted the woman. "If someone took a letter – and I can't think why you believe they did – then it could have been anyone in the house – one of the other girls, or one of the maids."

"I see – and then gave the letter to your husband? I really don't think your jury will believe that."

"What jury, Chief Inspector?" enquired the Solicitor. "You don't have anything to put before a jury – not a single witness."

"Have patience, Mr Wentworth. You see, there is something more. In each of the letters – written or rather typed – in English, there was a short line in Arabic. Now, in the fake letter there was a similar line. In English, it said '*I'm so proud of you'*.

"Now if, as you suggest, Mrs Livermore, your husband composed that letter, how would he know that Mr Hammadani habitually added a line in Arabic?

"And even more important, how would he know what to write? In this country, medical doctors are not often Arabic scholars, I think.

"But we aren't wasting time wondering about that, because we know how the line was created. You see, Mr Wentworth, a twelve-year-old girl in your client's house was given some lines as punishment. She just happens to be an Arabic speaker, and was told to convert them into Arabic 'because that will take you longer'. One of the lines was '*I'm so proud of you*'.

"Not, I think you'll have to agree, a line which a teacher issuing a punishment is likely to suggest. But I'm sure you will tell me that it's a complete coincidence that the exact same sentence was used in the fake letter."

There was silence for a few seconds.

"Has this witness made a statement?" asked Wentworth. Who is she?"

"Oh yes, she has made a statement; her name is Nadiyya Qadir."

"Ridiculous," snarled Mrs Livermore. "The girl is an out-and-out liar. Her evidence is worthless. She has made this up out of spite for me."

"Then explain this, Mrs Livermore. I

interviewed the girl in the presence of Inspector Davison and Miss Armstrong. At the time, nobody other than the police was aware of the existence of the letter, let alone details of the content. But when asked if anyone – unspecified – had asked her to translate anything into Arabic recently, she came straight out with this. And when asked what, again without any prompting she came up with three sentences. One of those just happened to be the sentence used in the fake letter. Another matter for the jury to consider."

"One witness, especially a twelve-year-old with a grudge, won't be sufficient, Chief Inspector."

"We do have a couple of other bits of what you will no doubt dismiss as 'circumstantial evidence', Mr Wentworth.

"First, Mrs Livermore, it seems that you telephoned your husband's partner, Dr Graves, on Monday, to inform him that Keith was suffering from influenza, and would be unable to work for a few days. I wonder why you decided to say that, when your husband had allegedly left a day or so earlier. If he had genuinely left you, you had no reason to think he wouldn't turn up for work. The reason for the lie will be quite obvious to the jury, I think. Would you care to comment?"

The woman glowered at the table, and didn't reply.

"There's something else, too. When my officers came to arrest you, they found several suitcases in the process of being packed – not just clothes but trinkets and other possessions from around your rooms. Were you thinking of going away on an unauthorised holiday in the middle of term? Or were you about to disappear with a hefty sum of ransom money, and move to a nice country with no extradition arrangements?"

Once again, Mrs Livermore said nothing. Wentworth looked somewhat uneasy. Adair continued.

"I'm sorry if I have given you both the impression that there is only one live witness. There is another, whose evidence, together with Nadiyya's and the circumstantial stuff, will certainly be sufficient to convict.

"You see, your husband has made a statement giving us chapter and verse about the whole thing – including your leading role. He'll be the chief witness for the Crown."

Mrs Livermore abruptly sprang to her feet and screamed. "The bloody rat! The idiot. It's all the Governors' fault – I should have been given the headship…"

"Shut up!" growled Wentworth, "you're doing damage."

"Too late, I fear," said Adair. "We did wonder about the motive – there really had to be something in addition to the money. So as well as what your husband euphemistically refers to as your pension fund, you get the satisfaction of probably ruining the school's reputation.

"Eleanor Livermore, I charge you with conspiring with Keith Livermore to commit the offence of kidnapping. I also charge you with being an accessory before the fact in the kidnapping of Megan Innes-Fielding and Aaliyah Hammadani. The Crown can decide later which one to proceed with. Or the indictment may be amended to one alleging simple kidnapping. We'll put you before a magistrate tomorrow.

"Take her back to the cells, Inspector."

The woman was now openly crying. She said nothing as Davison led her away. When they had gone, the Solicitor looked at the DCI, and gave a rueful grin.

"Ah well, I'd better start hunting for a barrister. Thinking about the wager you mentioned, Chief Inspector. It looks now as though the 'stout denial' horse isn't going to run. I don't know how you wagered, but I believe the bookies would say bets on a non-runner are void. It looks as though the 'cut-throat defence' may now be the odds-on favourite!"

The DCI laughed.

"Oh, I never thought the 'stout denial' would reach the starting line. And I might even hedge my bets, and risk a bob or two now on there being a second guilty plea – that might get your client two or three years off the fifteen or so she'll get on conviction!"

"No comment," replied Wentworth, "except to say that most counsel would prefer to have a goodly number of refreshers at say fifteen guineas per day, rather than live on a single fee!"

****

BOOKS BY THIS AUTHOR

The Bedroom Window Murder

Book 1 in the Philip Bryce series.

The Courthouse Murder

Book 2 in the Philip Bryce series.

The Felixstowe Murder

Book 3 in the Philip Bryce series.

Multiples Of Murder

Book 4 in the Philip Bryce series.

Death At Mistram Manor

Book 5 in the Philip Bryce series.

Machinations Of A Murderer

Book 6 in the Philip Bryce series.

Suspicions Of A Parlourmaid And The Norfolk Railway Murders

Book 7 in the Philip Bryce series.

This Village Is Cursed

Book 8 in the Philip Bryce series.

The Amateur Detective

Book 9 in the Philip Bryce series.

Demands With Menaces

Book 10 in the Philip Bryce series.

Murder In Academe

Book 11 in the Philip Bryce series.

Death Of A Safebreaker

Not in the Bryce series.

Death Of A Juror

Not in the Bryce series.

The Failed Lawyer

Not in the Bryce series.

Murder In The Rabid Dog

Book 12 in the Philip Bryce series.

The King's Bench Walk Murder And Death In The Boardroom

Book 13 in the Philip Bryce series.
To be published in 2025.

The Devon Murders

Book 14 in the Philip Bryce series.
To be published in 2025.

Printed in Dunstable, United Kingdom